WELCOME TO ANOTHER CRYSTAL LAKE PUBLISHING CREATION.

Thank you for supporting independent publishing and small presses. You rock, and hopefully you'll quickly realize why we've become one of the world's leading publishers of Dark and Speculative Fiction. We have some of the world's best fans for a reason, and hopefully we'll be able to add you to that list really soon. Be sure to sign up for our newsletter to receive two free eBooks, as well as info on new releases, special offers, and so much more. To follow us behind the scenes while supporting independent publishing and our authors, be sure to follow us on Patreon.

Welcome to Crystal Lake Publishing—Tales from the Darkest Depths.

OTHER NOVELS BY CRYSTAL LAKE PUBLISHING

House of Sighs by Aaron Dries

Beyond Night by Eric S. Brown and Steven L. Shrewsbury

The Third Twin: A Dark Psychological Thriller by Darren Speegle

Blackwater Val by William Gorman

Where the Dead Go to Die by Aaron Dries and Mark Allan Gunnells

Beatrice Beecham's Cryptic Crypt by Dave Jeffery

Aletheia: A Supernatural Thriller by J.S. Breukelaar

Sarah Killian: Serial Killer (For Hire!) by Mark Sheldon

The Final Cut by Jasper Bark

Pretty Little Dead Girls: A Novel of Murder and Whimsy by Mercedes M. Yardley

Or check out other Crystal Lake Publishing books for more Tales from the Darkest Depths.

THE MOURNER'S CRADLE

TOMMY B. SMITH

Let the world know:
#IGotMyCLPBook!

Crystal Lake Publishing
www.CrystalLakePub.com

Copyright 2018 Crystal Lake Publishing

All Rights Reserved

Property of Crystal Lake Publishing

ISBN: 978-1-64440-606-9

Cover Art:
Ben Baldwin—www.benbaldwin.co.uk

Layout:
Lori Michelle—www.theauthorsalley.com

Edited by:
Monique Snyman

Proofread by:
Lisa Childs
Amanda Shore

This is a work of fiction. Names, characters, businesses, places, events and incidents are either the products of the author's imagination or used in a fictitious manner. Any resemblance to actual persons, living or dead, or actual events is purely coincidental.

No part of this publication may be reproduced, stored in a retrieval system, or transmitted in any form or by any means, without the prior permission in writing of the publisher, nor be otherwise circulated in any form of binding or cover than that in which it is published and without a similar condition including this condition being imposed on the subsequent purchaser.

OTHER TITLES BY TOMMY B. SMITH

Poisonous

Pieces of Chaos (a short story collection)

Brought to you
by Crystal Lake
Publishing

Tales from The
Darkest Depths

1979
CEMETERY WHISPERS

EVEN BEFORE THE calamity that shook the city to its deepest foundations, St. Charles, a place of some charm and innocence during the late seventies, held its traces of dark history and secrets. As St. Charles expanded, becoming more actual city than town, its shadows subsisted. With industry and developments accelerating the city's way of life, many of the old tales, such as those surrounding Marion Cemetery, were forgotten by most.

"Be careful around Marion Cemetery," a few of the city's fading elderly used to say to their children. "Or the shadows might carry you away."

Dominguez remembered. Having seen almost a full century, he was a man of many secrets. Though his frame was frail and his mind aged, he remembered much.

As the cemetery's solitary gravedigger, Dominguez often strolled its outer perimeter during the dark hours. In his way, he walked the boundary of darkness and light.

His occasional whispering to the shadows punctured the silence, for two dark forms followed him closely.

Most other visitors to Marion Cemetery never saw the old whispering man with the deep-red ruby ring on his right hand. Some who came during the dark early hours heard his whispering, even if they did not see the man himself, and Lucy Newcomb was one such visitor.

On an autumn night of 1979, she approached a grave—a flat stone set in the dark-brown soil and surrounded by dried leaves that crunched with her approach. Dressed in a black coat with brass buttons, she came forward with a bouquet of sunflowers and daisies and laid them on the grave etched *Newcomb*.

The plain gray stone suited her aunt, simple in manner but kind at heart and gone for a year past.

Between the crunching leaves and the soft-blowing breeze, Lucy barely heard the whispering. She released the bouquet onto the stone and stood up straight. Anxious, she glanced around.

"Hello?" Lucy called, but the voice she thought she had heard went silent.

She looked at her aunt's grave again, then back to the darkness. Beyond a freshly-dug grave, she could discern nothing.

She made for the cemetery's black iron gates. Once past the gates and to the road which ran beside them, she hurried to the black Mercedes-Benz at the curb. She drove away, making only one more stop before leaving St. Charles.

Half an hour later, she sat in one of the small bars that clustered Candle Square. She didn't like the look of the place, but she wanted a drink. One drink turned into two. She couldn't shake the thoughts of the cemetery from her mind.

"Excuse me," she said to the gray-haired man behind the bar. He paused in the midst of wiping off a section of the bar with a white towel.

"Yes, miss?"

"What do you know about Marion Cemetery?" she asked him.

"What do you want to know? It's an old cemetery, the oldest in St. Charles. Lots of history in that place."

"Sure, there's history," said another man sitting two stools away from Lucy. "It's a cemetery." The man sipped his gin and tonic and added, "Those people in the ground, they're history."

The man had been sitting there for the past ten minutes, smoking his cigarette and drinking his drink beneath his brown mustache. A name tag pinned to the man's blue-collared shirt read *Mike*. Lucy glanced at him but didn't respond.

She looked back at the bartender. "I think I heard a voice there tonight. Someone whispering."

The bartender gave a slight nod, thinking. "You ought to be careful," he said. "You never know who might be wandering around in the cemetery at night." He finished wiping down the bar and moved along to another waiting customer at the opposite end.

As Lucy lifted her second Singapore Sling to her lips, she realized to her further discomfort that Mike still stared at her.

"So what did they say?" Mike asked.

"It was almost like he was watching me, whoever he was," Lucy said without looking up. "He was saying something like, 'Look at her, look how she breathes.

She's young. She probably has a healthy young heart, doesn't she?'"

"That's weird." Mike's gaze dipped toward the scuffed brown surface of the bar. He cracked open a couple of peanuts and popped them into his mouth.

"It was creepy." Lucy went back to her drink.

"Then what?"

"Nothing. I left after that."

Mike lit another cigarette. "It kind of sounds like a bunch of bullshit to me."

"How would you know?" Lucy exclaimed. "You weren't even there."

Mike didn't reply this time, already having lost interest. He finished his drink and went back to smoking.

Lucy gathered her things, paid her tab, and walked out. She left St. Charles soon afterward to move on with her life elsewhere. Likewise, the city went on without her.

LOSS

I

IN THE SPRING of '79, the efforts of Damon Sharpe's research reached a pinnacle. He had in part been victorious, he believed, in his battle to unearth a truth obscured by time. He had only to look on it with his own eyes to verify the success as more than personal, though it remained a victory few recognized as authentic.

The only things that made Damon different to his wife, Anne, were that she loved him and that he was who he was—and he had loved her, even if no one else seemed to remember her. *Damon's wife,* they probably called her, the ones who knew he had a wife. *The invisible woman.*

Spring became summer, which faded into early autumn. The leaves turned and fell.

Anne lay among the sheets of the bed with her head against a flat white pillow. As the wall clock ticked away, she stared at the empty space on the other side of the bed.

At the age of 38, her husband had died of a heart attack and Anne was alone with a house full of things, unfilled wishes, dreams, and remnants.

The days and hours became lost in a blur. Now she stood in silence in front of a polished wooden casket.

It might be the first time any of them had noticed Anne's wispy form, her light-complexioned features with pale blond hair that fell straight down on each side, and her brown eyes.

The others who filled the room spoke in hushed tones. Anne heard soft steps approaching from behind. A hand touched her shoulder. She pulled away from it.

"I'm sorry, dear," the person, an elderly woman with curled white hair, said.

"Sorry for what?" Anne replied. She saw no value in artificial kindness. She certainly didn't owe it to anyone.

She didn't even know the woman who stood in front of her or most of the rest of these people, and they never knew her. They couldn't know how she felt, what she and her husband had shared, or what remained now that he was gone.

The only things left of Damon Sharpe, other than the ring she wore and his still form in that casket, were inside of her and inside that house they had shared, though its contents had become almost worthless to her. The house might as well be empty. In a way, it was.

"Anne," a soft voice said to her from nearby, "if there is anything I can do, please let me know."

Anne turned and fixed the brown-haired woman in the gray dress with a flat stare. The woman swallowed, taking a step back.

"Anne, it's me," she said. "Tabby Reinhart. I know we haven't talked in a while, but—"

"Miss Sharpe?" another voice broke in, the voice of a man.

THE MOURNER'S CRADLE

The tall man in the dark blue suit stood just outside of Anne's peripheral vision, to her left and behind, as if he meant to force Anne to turn around to face him. She wouldn't give him that satisfaction. She continued to face the casket.

"My condolences," the man's low voice spoke.

"Why are you here?" Anne asked.

"Why, Miss Sharpe, I've come to pay my respects."

"There is nothing respectful about your visit here. We both know that."

The man shifted. She could imagine the amused look that crossed his face, even if she didn't look at him.

"Miss Sharpe—"

"*Mrs.* Sharpe."

A cough.

"Very well, *Mrs.* Sharpe, my name is Brock Keller. Your husband and I—"

"I know who you are," Anne said, "and I know why you're here. You're here to have one last laugh before they lower my husband into the ground."

She faced the black-haired man in the blue suit and locked him full in her stare. "You have no right to be here."

Keller appeared surprised. The surprise was feigned, Anne knew. No matter what he pretended or said to the contrary, Keller knew the hardship he had inflicted.

"You did your best to destroy everything my husband worked for," Anne said to him.

"No, Mrs. Sharpe, you have it wrong," Keller said.

"He was my husband," she said. "You think I don't know what went on in his life? You think I don't know about the things you've done? You're a liar, Keller."

Keller looked around, becoming nervous. People were staring. Tabby Reinhart, still standing near, took another step back.

"Get out of here," Anne said to Keller. "You are *not welcome here*. Get out."

"Don't you think you're overreacting?" he asked.

"Get out!" Her hand twisted into a fist. She swung and struck him right in the face.

Keller's head jerked back. His face flushed crimson. He grabbed her arms and she fought him, screaming.

"GET OUT! GET OUT!"

Arms grabbed Keller from behind and pulled him back. Tabby rushed between them, pleading quietly with Anne. Anne shoved her away. More people pulled Anne back, but she shouted and fought against them.

Keller yanked his arms free of those around him and strode for the door. At the door, he took a look back, his jaw clenched. His eyes burned with anger.

"Dear, please," the older woman urged Anne. "It's all right. He's gone."

Anne turned her eyes toward the door where Keller stood a moment before, saw the truth of the old woman's words, and forced her mouth shut. She pushed her shaking hands down to her sides.

"Will you be all right?" another voice asked her from out of eyesight. She didn't know who had spoken and didn't care. She took a deep breath. With this group of people around her, she felt like she was suffocating.

"Please," she said through her teeth. "I just need to be alone."

The group hesitated. After a moment, someone

stepped away. The rest soon followed, leaving Anne again to stand in front of her husband's coffin, tears on her face, emotion pouring from her fractured life.

The people standing behind her still wore those masks of concern, she imagined. She couldn't turn to face them. Not now, in her moment of weakness. They didn't deserve to witness this, her fragility. Besides, they wouldn't understand.

It wasn't sadness that possessed her and hardened her face against the tears that fell. It was hatred.

||

As far as Anne was concerned, the man who conducted the funeral didn't even know her husband, but he was the first one who had offered to conduct the service. When the generic eulogy dribbled from his lips, Anne sat looking but not quite listening. When it ended, she stood up and walked for the door.

"Honey, I'm sorry," someone said, and Anne moved right past her.

"Anne," a man with dark hair and eyes, who had sat in the back until now, called to her. His voice failed to penetrate her cyclone of thoughts. She ignored everything around her, especially those who tried to approach or speak to her, and continued walking until she met the cold, drenching rain outside. Thunder tore through the gray skies.

Ruben Ramirez emerged from the funeral home behind her, calling her name again, but Anne kept walking. The cacophony of torrents overcame all else until she reached the small gray car, put the key in, opened the door, and climbed in. She slammed the car door shut against the rain.

The drive home was a gray mess of rain-swept streets.

Once parked in her driveway, she walked again through the deluge with no hurry in her step. She unlocked the door and stepped into the house. Rainwater gushed from her clothing.

Anne's efforts to keep their home tidy despite Damon's accumulated stacks of books, paper-packed folders, and curiosities were hours wasted. Even with the clutter, the place seemed like a hollow shell instead of a home.

How different it appeared to her now. Everything familiar had become a mockery. She didn't think she could stay here any longer.

She found a black, blue-striped duffel bag jammed into one corner of the bedroom closet. She tossed it onto the bed and began throwing clothes into it.

Heedless of Anne's incredulity, the object of her late husband's studies persisted. Damon believed he had been close, but as close as he might have been, even he couldn't traverse the chasm that was death. After years of research, he would never see a resolution. He would never know for certain.

But Anne might. A strange idea had entered her distant mind while she sat quiet during the droning monologue of his funeral service.

Before the funeral, she considered burning every last one of his papers. Damon had been so consumed with it that it kept him from sleep on many nights. Even when he did slide into bed, insomnia kept him fidgeting for an hour or more. It drove Anne to annoyance until Damon sprang up again to continue reading and speculating on that mythological obsession of his.

He kept stacks of photographs. Anne had flipped through them but could never make full sense of them, which sometimes prompted a lengthy explanation from Damon. She did recognize photos of mounds of rock and crumbling stone structures from a Peruvian archaeological site. Some of the photographs were of rather random piles of rock elsewhere. She remembered a photo of a gourd painted with an obscure image and many more photos of *quipu,* those knotted strands of varying colors that remained of the ancient world. There were many more photographs in the attic, boxes of them.

Damon had also bought books—obscure, unlisted books. He had written enough to fill a book of his own, but that had never been his goal.

In the later days, Damon's sense of humor evaporated. His health waned. He became pale from too many hours indoors. He presented an odd sight in creeping through their home during the late hours in his efforts to keep from waking Anne, although she had already awoken. The ordeal had also taxed her.

A few men of influence had denounced Damon's work. His correspondence with archaeologist Dr. Lawrence Cornwell, who had exhibited a rare interest in Damon's discoveries, had become stagnant. Many of Damon's colleagues had turned their backs on him. Most of this, if not all of it, Anne attributed to Brock Keller. The man had the tongue of a snake.

Keller had done his part to make life difficult for Damon. Damon had nowhere else to turn for support but Anne, and also Ruben, whose assistance had proven useful on numerous occasions.

Anne liked Ruben. He didn't allow his emotions to get in the way of work. Anne might have been the same way, but today she proved to herself and others that she wasn't. When she saw Keller at the funeral, she lost it.

Without Damon in her life, Anne had a lot to consider and a massive decision to make. It might be the death of her.

She turned away from the bag on the bed, now stuffed with clothing, and moved around the bed to the oil painting on the opposite wall. Damon had painted it in his younger days; against a background of orange-yellow sunlight, it featured a row of birds' silhouettes perched on a fence. She slid the painting aside to reveal a wall safe.

She spun the combination dial through the proper sequence of numbers and opened the safe. Inside rested several stacks of cash and a folder thickly-padded with her husband's research papers.

Prompted by an impulse she couldn't place, Anne had left the folder in the safe before departing earlier for the funeral. Now she took the folder and every last dollar from the safe and transferred it into the duffel bag.

She no longer wanted to burn her husband's papers. She would keep them. Seeing Keller today had helped her to decide that. Damon was gone from her life, but Keller had shown his face today to prove he wasn't. Damon's work wasn't done. If that was the truth of it, Anne had a tremendous step to take.

There was one more thing: a camera. She found

Damon's camera, bundled it in multiple layers of soft cloth, and placed it into the bag.

After zipping up the bag, she thought about calling Ruben, but hesitated in front of the phone.

A thud startled her. Anne closed the safe and maneuvered the painting back into place.

Had the sound come from the front door? Was someone here? She sat on the bed beside her packed bag and waited for them to go away.

Outside, the rain continued to pour.

She heard something else, some other sound—a click? She leaned forward, listening, but found it difficult to hear between the rushing rain and her position in the back bedroom.

She walked to the living room and approached the curtained window to peek outside. Before she had the chance, she heard the sound again.

An unmistakable click sounded from the front door. She looked to the doorknob as it turned, and her heart pounded when the door swung open.

INTRUDER

I

WHEN THE MAN stepped in and saw her there, he froze. Their eyes locked.

He was bald, with a flat nose and narrow eyes. The beginnings of a gray-speckled black beard lined his jaw. His frame filled out a navy-blue tee-shirt and black jacket.

Anne broke away and ran. The intruder dashed after her. She reached the bedroom door and his hand twisted into the back of her shirt to jerk her backward. The clothing ripped. Thick gloved fingers seized her arm.

Anne spun and struck. Her knuckles struck his tender windpipe and he released her, shocked and gasping. He clutched his throat. Anne bolted into the bedroom.

She ran to the bag on the bed and grabbed for its strap but fumbled. The bald man charged through the bedroom doorway, running across the room toward her.

She turned and popped a vicious kick at him. Her heel glanced from his shin, and his weight slammed her to the edge of the bed. In her struggling, she slipped down to the carpet below. Her head struck the edge of the bed frame.

Dizziness spun her senses. Blood pounded in her ears. The man was on top of her, fighting to hold her down. She raised an arm to thrust for his eyes, but he pinned the arm. She screamed. He shoved a black-gloved hand over her mouth and slammed her head to the floor. She forced her jaws apart and bit deep, but scored only the leather of the thick glove.

He struck her in the side of the head. The smell of fear and violence filled Anne's senses. Darkness swirled around her. She fought the vortex that threatened to devour her consciousness.

Her right arm was pinned and so was the left, but she was able to work the latter free. She swung. The man pulled his head back and she missed. He swung in turn and drove a fist into her jaw.

She grabbed for something, anything, but there was only the night table on this side of the bed. She flung an arm upward and latched onto the handle of the night table's drawer. She yanked, and the weight of the drawer came free. It fell from her hand and toppled to the side. Paper and pens spilled out.

The man's arm shot out—to what, she couldn't tell—but her hand had already closed over one of the pens. She stabbed at his midsection, and hit her mark this time. He shouted. Anne stabbed again. He raised an arm and the pen's point stuck into his jacket sleeve. Whether it did any damage, Anne doubted, but the man rolled off her. She maneuvered her body into position to attempt another pen-jab, but the man had moved out of range.

She pulled herself up with no concern of grace. The

man, the front of his shirt darkening with blood, also came to his feet. Anne snatched up the duffel bag before the intruder rose completely, kicked him back off-balance, and sped out the bedroom door.

The man righted himself. He pulled out a switchblade, snapped out its blade, and moved after her.

Anne ran across the house to the open front door. She shot outside and flung the door shut behind her.

She went for the car with her keys in her hand. Her frantic motions missed the keyhole twice. Finally, she slid the key in and opened the door. She threw herself in, tossed the bag into the passenger's seat, and thrust the key into the ignition.

Through the heavy rain, she saw the front door of her house swing open. She started the car and revved the engine.

The man ran down the steps and toward the car, knife in his hand.

Anne shoved the car into reverse and sped backward. The man slowed when she curved back into the street. She shifted into first and shoved her foot against the gas pedal. Startled, the intruder almost stumbled backward when the car careened toward him. He ran back through the house's front door. Anne stopped the car on her wet front lawn.

The man showed his face from her front door, his eyes wild with menace. He still clutched the switchblade in one hand. He held his other hand to his bleeding abdomen.

Anne pushed the gas pedal again, driving the car in a circle around the front lawn until she reached the street. She sped away.

THE MOURNER'S CRADLE

Breathing heavily, the man walked back into the house. He closed the door behind him and lifted his shirt to inspect his wound. It was only flesh deep, but it bled.

He retracted the switchblade and picked up the phone, dialing a number on the pearly rotary. There was an answer on the second ring, but no voice spoke.

"I'm here at the house," the man said into the receiver.

"And?" a voice prompted.

"She was here," the man said. A drop of blood fell to the carpet. He pressed a gloved hand against his shirt. The puncture wound burned with the pressure. "She got away. She stabbed me with a pen, can you believe that? I couldn't stop her."

"Is there anything else?"

"That's it."

"Have you found anything?"

"I haven't had the chance to look."

"Make it quick. She'll probably call the police."

"Roger that."

The man hung up the phone and began ransacking the house.

II

The tires slid in the constant rush of water across the street. Anne gave the brakes a quick few punches and guided the car into the gas station's parking lot.

She checked her rearview mirror and peered out the car's windows to scrutinize the surrounding area before climbing out. She locked the car door and ran to one of the two pay phones arranged against a corner of the building.

She lifted the phone, saw a pink wad of chewed gum stuck to the receiver, and hung it up. She moved to the other phone. This one wasn't flawless, but without the gum, it was a winner. She dialed zero.

"Operator," came the answer.

"I need the St. Charles Police Department," Anne said. "It's an emergency."

"Hold on, please."

After a ring, a man's voice answered.

"This is the St. Charles Police Department," he said.

The unexpected violent encounter rushed back through Anne's mind, but she had no fear. She shook away the thoughts that attempted to bury her focus and replied, "This is Anne Sharpe. I was attacked earlier in my home."

"Miss, we'll need you to—"

"The man broke in through my front door," Anne continued. "He attacked me. I was able to get away. He might still be there. If you hurry, you might be able to catch him."

"Miss—"

Anne fired her home address into the receiver and hung up the phone. After a pause, Anne again picked up the phone, slid some change in, and tried to call Ruben.

It rang several times. Anne counted seven rings before hanging up.

With a glance at the yellow-lighted windows and glass door of the gas station, Anne walked away. She climbed back into her car, looked behind, and backed out. She drove through the persisting rain until she reached the lot's outlet and pulled onto the street.

She imagined the attacker from earlier, drawing in as much detail as she could muster; she envisioned his face, his clothing, that black jacket he wore, the gloves, and the brown hiking boots. His face had been covered with stubble. There might have been initial surprise in the man's eyes when he had seen her there, but she wasn't entirely certain. Still, if that was so, did it mean the man had not expected anyone to be present inside the home?

He had attacked her. What would he have done if he had succeeded in subduing her?

She shook her head. It didn't matter now, but she remained interested in the man. He had moved at a specific time: right after Damon's funeral. If Anne had gone with the rest of the procession to Damon's final burial at Marion Cemetery, she wouldn't have been home when the man came.

The more she thought of it, the greater her suspicions were that the man was no mere random thief. She needed somewhere to think. With the way her mind raced from one theory to another, she would be lucky not to run into a ditch, especially in this rain.

She looked at the duffel bag in the passenger's seat next to her. Her thoughts from earlier resurfaced. What she had been thinking then, could she carry through with it? Could she plunge deeper into Damon's fascinations than he himself had done?

Once she settled on her answer, the next question to come to mind was, *is this the exit or is it the next one?* Through the rain, she couldn't make out the sign until she was closer.

St. Charles Regional Airport, it read. She pulled off at this exit.

The rain lightened. When she reached the airport, Anne decided, she would try to call Ruben again.

TAKING FLIGHT

I

THE ST. CHARLES REGIONAL Airport was only semi-crowded today. Anne rushed across its expanse to the nearest pay phone she could find and dialed Ruben's number again. This time, he answered.

"This is Ruben Ramirez."

"Ruben, this is Anne."

"Anne. How are you?"

"I'm at the airport. Can you meet me here?"

"At the airport?"

"Can you meet me here or not?"

Ruben paused. Anne's voice had remained neutral, but her delivery was concise. She didn't care to squander the minutes away, not now. If anyone would understand, she thought, Ruben would.

"All right," Ruben said. "Tell me exactly where you will be and I'll meet you there."

"There is a café here," she said. "A small one in the airport. I think it must be new. I'll be waiting for you there. Is your passport current?"

"Excuse me?"

"If it is, bring it."

"What is this about, Anne?"

Finding a beginning wasn't easy. With everything coursing through Anne's mind, she ran the risk of spewing it out in an incomprehensible mess. "Ruben," she said after a moment's pause. "Can you just meet me at the café?"

Seconds of silence passed before Ruben spoke again. "I'll be on my way."

Anne hung up the phone. She walked along the expansive walkway, which was becoming more crowded now, toward the distant doorway on the right side, marked with an overhanging *Café* sign.

The small café was unoccupied except for the young man behind the counter. Anne ordered a cup of black coffee and had a seat at a table in the back corner. She allowed her coffee to cool and waited for Ruben.

Anne drank the coffee halfway down before Ruben arrived, dark hair, dark skin, dark eyes, dark collared shirt, and dark slacks. He saw Anne and came to the table.

He gave a brief, tight smile that said, *good to see you*, and pulled out the small, oval-shaped brown table's other wooden chair to sit across from her. He looked at her cup of coffee.

"I apologize that it took so long," Ruben said. "There was traffic and rain."

"I know," Anne replied. Her eyes moved down to her plain white coffee cup for a few seconds before she met his gaze again. "I'll be direct, Ruben. You worked with Damon for a long time."

"Yes?"

"You know he made discoveries that were discredited, but you also know who was largely responsible for this."

Ruben said nothing. He appeared uncomfortable and shifted his legs beneath the table.

"You of all people should know that if there had been a trace of doubt in Damon's mind, he would not have attempted to go public with the information. Are you aware of just how far he continued to pursue his studies even after Keller sabotaged his work and reputation?"

At the mention of Keller's name, Ruben's eyes went from Anne's coffee to a far wall of the café.

Anne continued. "Damon's discovery was hypothetical. I recognize that. He couldn't verify it for a lack of solid evidence, but he wouldn't be deterred. He was more than passionate. He was obsessed."

She leaned forward. "What interested him the most were the secrets buried with the ancient civilizations, the ones lost to the modern world. We know that evidence exists of Peruvian civilizations much older than the Inca and even the Chavín, but with no known written language and almost no art that we know of, there was very little left behind of these ancient cultures and we still have a lot to learn. Even to the end, Damon believed he was closer than many others to solving the mystery of a long-lost people."

Ruben looked up and across the table at Anne. "The Mourner's Cradle?"

"That was the term Damon used for it, yes." She regarded Ruben, put her hands around her coffee cup, and lifted it to take a drink.

Ruben looked at his watch. Anne felt a twinge of agitation. She set her coffee cup down with a hard clink, causing Ruben to glance up with mild surprise.

"Please don't waste my time, Ruben," Anne said.

"You should know better. While I understand that I'm not my husband, I do plan on finishing what he began."

"What do you mean?"

"Since you aren't being forthcoming and I don't know what it is you know and what you don't, I'll tell you. Damon believed he had pinpointed the location of that lost mystery, the one he called the Mourner's Cradle, to the eastern Peruvian mountainous region instead of the coastal area as first believed."

Ruben placed his hands on the edge of table. His eyes slipped down while he appeared to lapse into thought.

"Yes, I am aware," he said after a moment. "But why are you telling me this?"

"Because I'm taking a flight to Peru and I'm bringing my husband's documents with me."

Ruben paused, regarding her. "Doesn't that seem rather extreme?" he asked. An exaggerated calmness diluted his tone when he spoke.

Anne's lips were firm. "I couldn't care less what it sounds like to anyone else. When I finish my cup of coffee, I'm going to buy a plane ticket. My husband's journey in life might have ended, but his work isn't over. I'm still here. I know it was special to him and I want to know why. I want to understand."

"Of a lost civilization," Ruben said, shaking his head. "What do you think you will find that others haven't?"

"I have something that no one else has," Anne said. She lifted the bag beside her chair. "Damon's research papers are right here. He even has hand-drawn maps, one in particular that he was absorbed with over the last days, I remember. I'm bringing Damon's camera along. If I can find anything tangible at all, I'll have the pictures to prove it. I invited you here because I wanted to ask whether you wanted to come with me."

"Are you serious?"

"Don't I sound serious?"

Anne drank the last of her coffee. She stood, picked up the bag, and started away from the table. Ruben still sat, in thought.

Anne stopped and turned. "Ruben."

He looked over. "Yes?"

"I was attacked today in my home."

"What?"

"Have a nice day, Ruben. I'm going, with or without you."

She walked out.

She didn't have to wait in line for long. She stepped up to the counter, intent on the soonest flight that would carry her to her destination.

"When do you need to depart?" the woman asked her.

"As soon as possible."

"What time of day?"

"It doesn't matter."

"We have a flight leaving in a few days," the woman at the counter explained after checking on the matter. "Can you wait just a minute?"

Anne gave no response. She didn't want to stay in St. Charles another few days, but she appeared to have no other choice. She didn't want to go back to her house now, not after everything that had happened.

Anne considered staying at a hotel. She didn't want to spend any more money than was necessary. At the same time, she didn't treasure the thought of staying in some downtown hole-in-the-wall like the King's Motel or the Dollar Inn.

The woman at the counter turned away to speak to her superior, a thin, gray-haired man in a suit. Anne shifted her weight from one foot to the other, waiting and thinking about her unappealing options.

"Ma'am?" the woman said when the older man left her.

"Yes?" Anne responded.

"Today might be your lucky day."

Anne stared at her. It became obvious that this woman didn't know a thing about the day she'd had.

"As it turns out," the woman continued, "we now have some seats open on a flight just this afternoon, if you're interested."

"I'll take it," Anne said.

II

With the plane ticket in her hand, Anne checked her luggage, which was light, and found a seat in the open room to wait for her flight to board. Somewhere in the back of her mind, Anne had recognized the surety of this course from the moment she made that decision in the middle of her own husband's funeral. She only now admitted it to herself. She was bound for Peru with nothing but her own determination, her husband's writings and sketchings, his copies of documents and photographs, and his camera.

The tales of the lost world had diminished to scattered remnants. Some of these Damon had obsessed to decipher. He was resourceful and had a way of crafting situations to his benefit. He had certainly made the right connections, at least in the beginning, and this lent him access to discoveries and reports unreleased to the general public.

Anne remembered their trip to South America well. Damon had remained busy, but he emerged galvanized in his efforts for reasons Anne didn't understand. Instead of quenching his desire for immersion in the obscure details of those dead legends, as Anne had hoped, the venture had deepened his thirst for that knowledge.

The turning point, she suspected, was the day when Damon's exploration led him to a dirt-floored hut and its elderly resident, a thin, bald-headed man. He sat on the floor, mumbling at times so that even Damon had difficulty understanding him.

"What is he saying?" Damon had asked the other younger man, the man's impassive nephew.

"La cuna de luto, mister—what is your name? Sharpe, you say?"

La cuna de luto. An odd name, the Cradle of Mourning, linking birth with death— what did it mean?

Anne wished they hadn't spoken to that batty old man, listening to his riddles and dead-end tales.

The later discovery of alternate tales, crude folklore and legends betrayed by a handful of the old or wandering mad reinforced Damon's suspicions of an ancient grave site, though there was no recorded information of its existence until Damon's final research paper. There Damon recounted it by name, "The Mourner's Cradle."

Among all of the papers she brought, Anne also

had the notes Damon made prior to his passing. These had never seen publication or dismissal in any form. In these final notes, Damon had pinpointed, as closely as he thought he or anyone else ever might, the location of that hypothetical mystery in the western Andes.

With bits of this information committed to memory and contained in the duffel bag that rested beside her in the airport waiting area, Anne would make the first focused effort to locate some sign of the Mourner's Cradle.

As she fidgeted with the plane ticket in her hands and thought about the journey ahead, someone sat down beside her. She looked up and saw Ruben. She looked back to the plane ticket without speaking.

"You're really doing this, then," Ruben spoke, not as a question. Anne said nothing.

"I shouldn't let you do this," he added, his tone quiet. This drew Anne's glance.

"What makes you think you would be able to stop me?" she asked.

Ruben released a sigh. His head dipped. "All right. You have me."

"What does that mean?"

"I'm here," he said. "I'm listening. I'll do what I can to help you, but—" He paused. "I want you to understand, I can't do it for free. Damon was my friend, but he was also an associate."

"Fine, Ruben."

Ruben rubbed his palms against his pants. He raised his head, and his eyes roamed toward the windows, a distance beyond which he could see the waiting plane.

"You told me you were attacked," Ruben said. "What happened to you?"

"There isn't time," Anne said. "My flight boards soon. I'll be traveling to Lima and heading east from there. If you're planning on coming with me, you should buy a ticket."

"Lima," Ruben echoed.

"I'm going to find out what I can."

"Are you sure you will find anything?"

"No, I'm not sure of anything."

"I wish you would reconsider, but I suppose I shouldn't leave you to do this alone."

"Then buy a ticket. They have a few seats left on a flight this afternoon, or they did. If you're going to buy a ticket, you should do it now."

Ruben wiped his hands on the front of his pants again and stood. He glanced at Anne once more before walking away.

The airport attendant called Anne's flight. She stood with her plane ticket in her left hand and the strap of the bag draped around her right arm, and walked across the gray-carpeted floor to the attendant. She showed her ticket. The woman motioned her past.

When the attendant called for the last time, Ruben came hurrying along with his ticket.

III

Sometime before the blue uniforms and blue lights appeared in front of the Sharpe home, Vince was gone from the house. He now stood in downtown St. Charles, not far from Candle Square, speaking on a pay phone.

"Nothing?" the voice on the other end asked.

"Nothing," Vince said. With the black receiver of the pay phone pressed near his crusty lips, he glanced around. "I turned the house upside down, couldn't find a thing. She had to have taken it all with her."

A hard gust of wind blew cold rain across Vince's jacket and face. He turned away from it and toward the pay phone, awaiting further instructions.

On the other end of the phone line, Keller had lapsed into silence. He paced the white tile of the foyer dressed in the same blue suit he had worn to Damon Sharpe's funeral. In contrast to Vince's miserable surroundings, Keller stayed warm and dry in his home, but he was far from satisfied.

It had been his own fault, Keller realized, for underestimating Anne Sharpe. Now she was gone, but to where?

He would need to make some more calls to get to the root of the situation, but he had his suspicions. After recent events, Mrs. Sharpe was either going into hiding somewhere in St. Charles or she was leaving town. If she left, where would she go?

Letting the situation lie was no longer an option. Anne knew Vince's face now. Vince's actions could be traced back to Keller, and the law could become involved.

"Vince, I need you to wait where you are," Keller said. "I need to make a few calls." Before Vince could answer, Keller hung up the phone.

Left cold in the rain, Vince pulled his jacket tighter around himself. He looked across the rainy parking lot, at the vehicles whizzing in and out of it. More rain, carried by the wind, splashed him. He leaned against

THE MOURNER'S CRADLE

the wall and turned his face from the rain as best he could.

Vince heard footsteps above the sound of the rain. He lifted his gaze to see a man approaching.

"Sir, are you using this phone?" the man asked, since Vince was blocking the pay phone. "I need to make a call."

"Beat it," Vince said.

The man stared, sizing Vince up. Vince reached into his jacket.

"You don't want to start something you can't finish," Vince said to the man. His gloved hand closed around the switchblade in his jacket.

The man muttered something under his breath and turned to leave.

"That's what I thought," Vince said. He waited, keeping an eye out for anyone else who might come around to challenge his stance in front of the phone. Next time, he wouldn't be so nice about it. His stomach hurt where that bitch had stabbed him earlier. He'd pay her back for it, no question about that.

While Vince waited in the cold dampness, Keller stepped into the cozy study of his home and picked up the phone.

If Anne Sharpe was still in St. Charles, he would find her. He knew people. He might not find her today, but eventually, he would find her. After that incident at the funeral, his pride wouldn't allow otherwise, and that wasn't the whole of it.

The Keller family pride was a hefty inheritance. Brock Keller was the last of the line. He knew what failure could do to a Keller.

His father had led the failed Keller Expedition into

those frozen Antarctic burrows where many had perished, and the hardships were for naught. Damon Sharpe's work had been a considerable part of that venture.

Keller had watched the heavy failure drive his father into a bottle, where he deteriorated for the rest of his days, his reputation and finances ruined. The deaths suffered during that wasted trek were on Old Man Keller's head, and he had paid dearly.

Seeing his father reduced to such a self-pitying wreck wasn't easy. During the old man's drunkest moments, he had a few choice words about Damon Sharpe. Keller had listened. The genuine anger in his father's voice had commanded his attention. It remained the only aspect of his father's emotional breakdown he could respect, and he remembered it well after his father's death.

Brock Keller was a different sort of man than his father. If someone struck him, he struck back harder. Sometimes, he struck first.

Keller became intrigued when Dr. Cornwell saw value in Damon Sharpe's later work. How could Cornwell find any respect for Damon Sharpe, a charlatan who couldn't keep his facts in order?

If Sharpe's work really interested Dr. Cornwell, Keller thought, the man needed a hard dose of reality. At the same time, he realized that if Sharpe actually *had* made a discovery of note, he owed it to his old man to take Damon Sharpe down and stick the knife in deep.

Among other things, Keller had informed Cornwell of Damon Sharpe's involvement in the Keller Expedition. By making a few calculated phone calls,

Keller ensured much of Sharpe's so-called "research" was exposed as unreliable, useless, even dangerous as evidenced by the Keller Expedition.

Keller called it justice. He only wished his father could have lived to see it.

You shouldn't ever cross a Keller. Damon found that out. His bitch of a wife would learn the same.

Keller had tossed around the notion of confiscating Damon Sharpe's final unpublished research materials, both to satisfy an unshakable curiosity and as a final clump of dirt onto Sharpe's coffin. Only after that confrontation in the funeral home had he truly set his mind to the task. A call to Vince hadn't taken long, but he hadn't anticipated Anne's early return. Regardless, Keller would remedy the situation.

After speaking to Rochelle at the St. Charles airport, Keller found the answer he searched for. Anne Sharpe had made a decision that was either very brave or stupid.

Keller called Vince back. "Yeah," the man's voice, like sandpaper, coughed into the phone.

"Vince, we have a flight to catch."

"Mind if I ask where to?"

"Lima."

"Where?"

"Lima, Peru. I'll call you back when I have more information. I'll have to secure us a flight. They're telling me that all of the flights are booked but I can pull a few strings. Just be somewhere where I can reach you and don't do anything suspicious."

"Roger that," Vince replied.

Keller hung up. He left his study to prepare for the trip ahead.

Out in the rain, Vince clicked the greasy black public phone onto its receiver, shoved his hands into his pockets, and shuffled away.

LIMA

I

RUBEN MANAGED TO convince the random flyer next to Anne to trade seats with him. Soon, the plane hummed along the runway stretch, lurched upward, and lifted them into the skies.

Anne wasn't speaking much. Ruben had a glass of water and ignored the package of peanuts brought. Halfway through the flight, Anne's near-silence abated.

"Ruben," she said to him, "Keller showed up at my husband's funeral."

Ruben nodded. He kept his eyes on the back of the seat in front of him.

"I know," he said. "I was there."

"Of course," Anne said with a sigh. "I'm sorry."

Ruben had seen what had happened with Keller. Everyone had. Anne wished he hadn't, although she wasn't ashamed of it.

"It's all right," Ruben said quietly. "I realize we never spoke there. I was trying to give you some space. I could tell that was what you wanted. I tried to speak to you on your way out, but I don't think you even heard me. You were already out the door and it was raining hard."

"Thank you for being there."

Ruben didn't say anything. He didn't have to.

"After I went home, I was attacked."

She related the full story to him along with the man's description. Ruben shook his head but didn't say much more. He was relieved that she had come out of it without suffering serious harm, although his worry was clear when he looked closer and saw the bruise on one side of her jaw. She brought her hand to the area and prodded the tender spot.

"If you need anything, please ask," Ruben said. "I have aspirin."

Anne turned forward again, cast her eyes downward, and shook her head. Inwardly, she knew she should be grateful. She had asked a lot in hopping aboard a flight to Peru on a moment's notice. How many others would have even considered it?

Ruben didn't have a family, only an ex-wife. Nonetheless, Anne had expected some polite form of *no* from him. He had surprised her. He was here for her as he had been for her husband and at least she could be glad she still had *someone*.

When the flight landed, Anne was quick to fetch the luggage, or as quick as she could be since the Jorge Chávez International Airport was clogged with tourists. Ruben offered to assist with the luggage, but there was little enough that Anne didn't need the help. She picked it up and continued walking. Ruben trailed behind her.

A man's eyes latched onto them from the crowd. He made rapid steps to cross their path. Anne stopped. Ruben almost bumped into her from behind.

"Anne?" the man asked with a smile. Startled, Anne studied the man's unfamiliar face.

"Do I know you?" she asked at last.

"Your name is Anne?" the man asked. "Anne Anderson?"

"Anderson? No."

"Sorry," the man apologized. "A mistake. Have a good day." He moved out of their way and pushed into the crowd, disappearing.

Anne glanced back at Ruben, who shrugged. The two resumed moving through the crowd with slow but gradual progress.

In another part of the airport, the man who had seemingly mistaken Anne's identity found another man dressed in brown slacks and a gray collared shirt. "Javier," he said, drawing the man's gaze, and pointed toward the departing forms of Anne and Ruben.

Javier gave the man a nod and a push in that direction. The man left, hurrying after Anne and Ruben toward the airport doors. He pushed through the bunch blocking his path and, from a safe distance, followed Anne and Ruben out to the streets.

II

A leap of impulse brought Anne and Ruben to Lima, but the city was far from their destination. When Ruben ventured talk of the city's wealth of museums and theaters, Anne met this with a sigh. Ruben probably meant it as a distraction, but Anne couldn't muster a lot of enthusiasm for the conversation.

She had no eyes now for the *Museo Larco* or any of the other wonders of the city as Ruben's first wandering interest suggested. She had seen enough during her previous visit with Damon, and Ruben had not been fortunate enough to accompany them then.

At Anne's lack of a response, Ruben sank into silence again. Anne continued to lead the way, now to a modest lodging establishment.

From a street away, their pursuer watched.

Their room was small, scented of balsam with walls of deep-brown. Two beds furnished the room, both covered with light-brown linens.

Anne dropped the duffel bag and sat on the edge of one bed. She lowered her face into her hands. Ruben eased the door shut.

Anne raised her weary eyes. "I feel so exhausted," she said, "but I couldn't possibly sleep now."

Ruben sat on the other bed. "Can I get you anything?" he asked.

"Why are you doing this?"

"What do you mean?"

"You must think I'm insane. Why are you here with me?"

"Damon was a friend," Ruben said, "and so are you. Your husband and I worked together, but he was also a friend to me during difficult times. My divorce—remember?"

Anne nodded.

"Very messy," Ruben said. "My fault, I admit. Too much drinking and gambling. Damon, he never judged me for my mistakes. That's the true test of a friendship, I think. When things are at their worst, your friend is still there."

Anne's hands twisted together in her lap. She couldn't say she understood this enduring loyalty of Ruben's.

"Ruben," she ventured.
"Yes?"
"I'm glad you came."

He answered her with a meek smile. Little more was said.

Outside, an observer waited for several more minutes before withdrawing.

III

Anne didn't care to wait in the city for long. On Ruben's insistence, she agreed that it wouldn't be wise to fling herself down a path across the Peruvian countryside and into the mountains without a well-suited source of knowledge of the terrain and potential obstacles. To her surprise, Ruben soon found a man willing to help.

His name was Raul, and he was an experienced mountaineer. Raul, as it happened, would be returning to his home of Huancayo soon. He would carry on with them further into the Andean region for a price which was considerable but also understandable.

"It is a strange journey to make," Raul remarked, "and for the place you want to reach, it might be dangerous."

"Danger I can handle," Anne said. She had a brief thought of the break-in incident back in St. Charles.

"Good," Raul said. "Because by dangerous, I mean expensive, too."

"Of course," Anne sighed.

"If you will pay what I ask, and you know the risk, we have a deal. I will need to have payment up front."

"He seems genuine," Ruben said to Anne on their

way back. "Probably the best we'll find. We are lucky to have found him. There was no time to check references. This is all very spur-of-the-moment."

Anne and Ruben returned to their rooms to clear out their belongings and make the final preparations for departure.

"I don't know how you did it," Anne said to Ruben, slinging a pack over her shoulder. "Finding Raul, I mean. I don't know how I could have managed this by myself."

"I'm sure you would have found a way," Ruben replied, still packing.

"Maybe."

"Lima is a big city," Ruben said. "If there is anything we need, we can probably find it here. After we leave, things might be different."

Ruben hefted his pack and the two of them walked out, back down the stairs to the ground level and out to meet Raul.

When they arrived at the street corner, Raul already stood waiting. He raised a hand to distinguish himself from the others clustered around. Without much ado, the three left to catch a ride in a beaten old green van, something else Ruben had taken the trouble to arrange.

Dubious, Anne climbed in after the other two. Soon they rolled along, heading eastbound and leaving the bustling streets of Lima behind.

IV

Another plane lowered onto the airport strip. On board were Brock Keller and a man named Vince.

After the flight settled and they moved out with the rest of the passengers, Vince gathered their tow of luggage. Keller met the man who waited for them.

"Good day," he said. "You must be Mr. Keller."

"I am," Keller said.

"My name is Javier." Javier rubbed his dark-whiskered chin and studied Keller from his eyes down to his blue suit.

"I trust all was discussed between you and our mutual friend?" Keller asked.

Javier continued to scrutinize Keller for several seconds before answering with a nod. "Yes, Mr. Keller. All is quite clear." He diverted his eyes for an instant, but jerked his gaze back to the forward position when Vince approached with two briefcases and a travel bag in tow.

"Who is this?" Javier asked.

"This is Vince," Keller said. "Another of my associates."

"Is there anyone else?"

"No, just the two of us."

Javier took another quick glance around. "Forgive me, Mr. Keller," he said, "but it is best that we move quickly. You have a serious job for us, I understand. We should leave here to continue our discussion in private."

Keller nodded. "Come along, Vince."

Keller walked after Javier toward the airport's exit. Vince followed behind them, pushing his steps to keep up despite his load.

STRANGERS

I

THE VAN RIDE wasn't pleasant. The driver seemed to plow through every single bump and dip in the road. Anne's bones jarred with each bounce. She clenched her teeth and fired a glare at Ruben, but he already knew her agitation. He kept looking out the window in the opposite direction.

While Anne and Ruben sat in the back of the van, Raul was in a seat in front of them. He made occasional quiet exchanges with the other two at the front.

The vehicle's driver was a large man with a shaved head who spoke almost entirely in grunts. The other man, who sat in the passenger's seat, was a skinny man with a bunched wad of dark curly hair on top of his head. The driver kept his eyes on the road. The other man kept turning his head toward the back of the van and looking at Anne a bit too often.

Anne was grateful when they rolled into Huancayo. She climbed out with Ruben and Raul. Raul went to business with assembling supplies for their journey. Ruben went with him. Anne also decided to go along, but stayed out of their way. It didn't take long for her to decide she wanted no part of the haggling and arguing Raul seemed to dive into during every exchange.

Raul was crude, shouting, cursing, and belittling the merchants. When he concluded the moment's business, he turned back to Anne and Ruben and his previous pleasantness returned in an instant. Raul had the ability to berate someone like a trash-eating dog one minute and shake hands with a smile the next.

Raul led them to another street corner where a smaller white hatchback vehicle with chipped paint and rust spots waited for them. Raul and Ruben loaded in their olive-green supply packs which were cram-packed with supplies of new climbing gear, food fit to last for their travel, and assorted other items.

Raul climbed into the passenger's seat. Ruben and Anne squeezed into the back.

Their driver was an amiable gentleman this time, someone Raul seemed to know from frequent dealings in the past. They chatted in the front while Anne sat in silence, looking around at the torn upholstery and dirty windows. Ruben stared ahead.

Even if the dirty car smelled like stale sweat, at least the drive wasn't as bad this time around. Anne peered between the two in the front and tried to look through the front windshield. She couldn't see much because of the smudged glass.

Raul noticed her leaning forward. He turned his head to one side and regarded her from the corner of an eye.

"Once we are on foot," he said to her, "we will still have a long way to go. Are you ready?"

"I'm as ready as I'm ever going to be," she replied. "It's too late to turn back now, don't you think?"

Raul gave a nod. He donned his polite smile.

"This will not be easy," he said, "but don't worry. I will do my best."

They were deposited on foot somewhere along a narrow road in the middle of who-knew-where. Anne heaved a supply pack onto her back and secured it in place. In her arms she carried another bag, the duffel bag she had brought from her home in St. Charles.

As the car departed, they left the road on foot by Raul's direction. He led them across the green land until it darkened with the sun's falling. When night surrounded, Raul stopped to unload his gear.

"We will need our rest," he explained, "and food. It is important that we take care of ourselves. When we reach the mountains . . ."

Raul gave a shake of his head, as if this was enough of an explanation in itself. Over the next half-hour, they unpacked and set up camp.

At first, Anne was apprehensive. Taking a night's rest out here under the stars, so vulnerable, didn't appeal to her.

Was it that her mind kept wandering back to that incident in St. Charles when she was attacked in her own home? She wasn't certain, but she knew she didn't feel safe anymore.

Inside the tent, with Raul and Ruben right outside, Anne succumbed to a broken, troubled night's sleep. She opened her eyes several times in the night and listened, only to hear the random nocturnal sounds of nature, the skittering of a small animal, or the mournful wailing of birds.

II

The morning saw a quick meal of bread and sour cherry jam accompanied by cups of black coffee. "Any sleep?" Ruben asked Anne.

"Not much," Anne replied, her hair a mess as she sat huddled over her cup of coffee. After breakfast, the three broke down the camp for a prompt continuation of their journey.

The great mountains towered in the distance. For countless steps, that distance remained vast, the mountains appearing to come no closer. Anne did herself no favors by keeping her eyes on the horizon throughout much of the trek. When the signs of a village came into view, this gave the monotony and her thoughts an initially welcome diversion.

A couple of men sat with their backs against the wall of a tiny, worn brown house. Both of them stared. Another man farther along the road smoked a hand-rolled cigarette and watched their every movement. When they met the stares, the dark eyes were flat and unreadable.

"What is this place?" Ruben asked Raul. Raul shook his head.

"They are suspicious of strangers here," Raul said, managing to avoid Ruben's question altogether.

Ruben didn't press the inquiry. He decided in kind with Anne that if this place had a name, it didn't matter.

Anne drew more stares than the two men with her. With her contrast of such lighter features, she stood apart. For another, she was a woman, the only one around, as far as she could see—and not a typical one at that.

She didn't allow it to bother her. She didn't plan on staying here long.

She focused her attention on the horizon. She could see the mountain expanses, standing majestic, brown and trailed with white.

Ruben's eyes followed her gaze. He made no effort to conceal the doubt that reentered him at the sight of the grand peaks. The heavy reality of their journey penetrated the silence between them.

Anne looked to their guide. "Raul, have you ever heard anything about an ancient graveyard somewhere up there in the mountains?"

She wasn't sure "graveyard" was the correct term, given the obscurity of what she sought, Anne knew, but why not ask?

Raul drew his eyebrows together, puzzled. "In the area we are traveling? No. Why do you ask?"

Anne shook her head. She didn't feel like explaining right now. She lifted the duffel bag by its strap, which she had looped around her hand. "It isn't known to most people. I thought I should ask, though, since you've traveled this way before."

"No," Raul said.

"How many others have you guided along that specific route?"

"I am not sure," Raul said. "None that I remember. But don't worry. I will get you there."

Anne saw that most of the people were still watching her, though some had gone into their homes or other buildings.

"That's reassuring, Raul," she responded at last. "And helpful."

III

On the road, Javier said to Keller, "There will be a price."

"Of course," Keller responded with some flippancy. "There always is."

Javier glanced at the man. "This is an important matter to you," he assessed.

"I wouldn't waste my time otherwise," Keller said.

Javier's dark eyes studied Keller. Keller hadn't made a detailed explanation of the reasons for the job, but he was a paying client, and his money was good. In most cases, this proved sufficient.

Anne's flight to Lima only solidified Keller's hunch that Damon Sharpe, through his research of the lost Peruvian treasures, had known something of value, or at least strongly believed he had. Even if Sharpe was dead, Keller wasn't prepared to afford the man another victory.

Remembering his father's failure was like picking at a scab. The thought of Damon's wife securing some final redemption for her husband's work sickened him like an infection working beneath.

Thinking of it brought a lethal compound to simmer within. More flashes of memory assaulted him. He remembered his father's drunken tears, then his death. He remembered standing in that blue-carpeted funeral parlor where Anne Sharpe had hit him right in the face. Keller clenched his teeth at the memory.

Javier still watched Keller. He saw the cold steel that came into his eyes. He knew the look. This wasn't a mere business trip.

"I understand, in my way," Javier said. While his tone was pleasant, no smile touched his face. "Some things are personal. I assure you, Mr. Keller, if you can meet my price, I will not allow them to slip away from us."

"Good."

Well after Anne, Ruben, and Raul had departed from the small village, pushing toward the mountains, the three men arrived along the course of their own journey. Their clothes were rumpled. They traveled light. They had sacrificed most notions of comfort for the sake of haste.

"You've done a good job tracking them," Keller said to Javier. "I'll make sure you're well-compensated for your work."

Javier gave no reply. He scrutinized their surroundings and the people who watched them.

The staring made Vince uncomfortable. He shifted on his feet, watching the people of the village, and reached into his jacket for the reassurance of his switchblade.

"From what you have told me," Javier said to Keller after some delay, "I believe I know which way they have gone, but we should do some asking. The people here must have seen them pass through."

"Do you think any of them will talk?" Keller asked.

"They will," Javier said, "once I make them."

Javier put a hand into his light jacket and unsnapped a pistol from its leather shoulder holster. His hand closed around the cold weapon, his finger resting against its trigger.

MOUNTAINS

I

THEY DREW NEARER. The mountains appeared larger, much larger, than they had from that distance of hours before. Soon, they seemed incredible and immense, dwarfing Anne, Ruben, and Raul to tiny specks of near-nothing. Was this a fool's errand or a suicide climb?

And it hadn't even started yet.

Ruben glanced over at Anne. "Are you sure about this, Anne?"

She didn't return his glance. "Am I sure? This is hardly the time for second thoughts."

Anne noticed the doubt in Raul's expression when he glanced toward her, even as he tried to hide it beneath an overly-patient smile. He didn't give Ruben that same smile, she noticed. She guessed Raul had never embarked on this sort of climbing venture with a woman. If this concerned the man, Anne decided, she shouldn't bother herself to care. Between her husband's death and the undertaking before her, she would do it anyway, all else be damned. No obstacle would stand in her path.

They plodded and climbed across rocky terrain.

They bypassed numerous jagged rocks and boulders in their path of travel to the north, skirting the mountain's perimeter. Anne and Ruben looked upward to the powerful, looming sight of the mountain before them, and it did nothing to lighten their spirits.

They traveled through the day across the brown and gray rocks. In time, a light rain pattered down around them. A dirty gray mist infiltrated the air.

Raul moved past Anne and Ruben into the lead. He produced a small compass, checked it, surveyed their surroundings, and tucked the compass away. They kept moving. For the remainder of the next hour-and-a-half, none of the three spoke. Anne withdrew to her thoughts.

Did this Mourner's Cradle even exist? Possibly not. In the great scheme of things, Anne recognized beneath the overwhelming mountain, she didn't know much of anything.

Her mind roamed into the disheartening likelihood that she chased a foolish whim, but as she had previously asserted, it was too late to turn back now. If her husband had toiled for disillusion, she would scale the mountain and confront that enlightened disappointment in his place.

At the base of the mountain, Raul stopped, holding up a hand. "We start climbing here," he said, and turned to face them. "It is best we get ready."

Ruben set his pack down on the rocks, opened it, and began pulling out wads of clothing and climbing equipment, which he set to one side. Observing Ruben, Anne did the same.

After a quick round of instructions from Raul, they geared up accordingly. Anne moved behind a mound

THE MOURNER'S CRADLE

of rocks to change as all three stripped away the old clothing and transitioned into the bulkier, more insulating wear. Anne removed her wedding ring and shoved it into the bottom of the duffel bag.

Once finished, they crammed the rest of their unused articles back into the supply packs and confronted the mountain.

II

Over the next hour, the temperature plunged. A layer of snow became visible. Some distance higher, ice crunched beneath their upward steps. The wind whistled into their ears, which were at least shielded by the hoods of their thick coats.

Rope connected them. The crampons affixed to their boots offered the relief of additional traction when the climb's slant steepened.

Each of them wore one of the green supply packs, and Anne continued to carry the bag containing her husband's documents and camera, as well as her wedding ring. She had looped it around one shoulder. Ruben thought this was a bad idea, but he hadn't tried to argue with her about it for long. Both knew he wouldn't have made any progress if he had.

The climb became a rigorous vertical ascent. Soon, their gloved hands gripped ice axes, cracking them into the ice repeatedly until Anne's muscles burned from the effort.

Between the exhausting labors of the climb, she had little room to sort out how much time elapsed during their fight up the mountain. Would the entire climb be this difficult?

Ruben had some past recreational climbing experience. It wasn't much in the face of these treacherous mountains. Raul had the true experience here. They heeded his instructions to the letter.

A sense of relief came when they saw a ledge some distance above. Raul climbed onto it first, helping Ruben and then Anne up to the stretch of standing ground. Anne and Ruben stopped here to gaze out to the rough curve of brown-and-white landscape below.

The harsh wind chapped one side of Anne's face. She attempted to huddle away from it, and it slung her sandy blond hair across her eyes. She sighed and reached up with gloved fingers to brush the tangled hair back. When the wind relented, she turned to see Raul standing against the mountain wall and Ruben looking out from near the brink of the ledge.

Holding her hair back from the wind-frenzy with one hand, Anne walked toward Ruben. She took another glance to the rocky lands far and wide below.

"We're a long way from St. Charles," she said.

"I hope this is worth it," he said. He lifted his eyes to the sky. "It's getting dark. Soon it will be worse up here."

Anne shifted in the snow. Ruben walked past Raul and surveyed the area above.

"I guess we've waited here long enough," he said.

They resumed the climb. The winds attacked them with renewed ferocity.

Anne hammered her axe into the ice, focusing on the areas Raul and Ruben had gripped before her. Her muscles burned against the coldness. Her breaths became shorter and more rapid, she noticed. She felt a touch of lightheadedness, but pushed herself to continue the climb.

Years before, Anne reflected, long before Damon's dedication to the Mourner's Cradle had commenced, she and Damon had maintained a regular fitness routine. They often took a morning run and sometimes a longer bicycle ride on the weekends. There had been a few hiking trips, a couple of which were along mountain trails. She remembered doing some rock-climbing then, but it counted for little in comparison to this feat.

Then there was that heavy red punching bag, acquired in used condition from an estate sale during the later days. Damon seldom used it. By that time, he had already been ostracized by the archaeological and historical research communities, and he remained far too busy with his work.

He had reason to worry. The past had returned to destroy him.

His research had supplanted the Keller Expedition, a grievous mistake, and this example was dredged from the past, hefted high, and emblazoned in bold across every page of Damon's dossier. As a result, funding became nearly impossible. Cornwell, with whom Damon had reached an informal agreement on a true exploration of the possibility of the Mourner's Cradle, withdrew.

Both Damon and Anne knew the source of their distress. Its name was Brock Keller.

Damon's hours of study had multiplied. Many of his other activities diminished, abandoned in favor of work. During that time, Anne struck the heavy bag plenty of times, often until her knuckles were almost as red as the bag. When she rode her bicycle, she sometimes strayed off the standard course, pushing hard until the exhaustion hit her and forced a slow, inevitable return home.

Her harsh physical rigors had been an outlet for her frustrations. At least they had helped to keep her in decent shape. She couldn't imagine how much more difficult the day's climb might be otherwise.

Powdery snow pelted down from the others climbing above. Anne blinked and lowered her head to keep the falling snow from her eyes.

Chafed by the coldness, the strain of the climb, and the uncertainty, Anne's thoughts pushed against the haze of time for another faraway place. Only days before that, her husband sat in the chair of their storage room, which had transformed into his private study. He sat surrounded by stacks of books, writing, working, internalizing.

What had she said to him? Had they even exchanged words that night?

She had brought him a drink as he worked, a glass of cola with ice. He took the drink and leaned against her. Their eyes met as innumerable times before. Words seemed unnecessary.

She went to bed. The next morning, he was gone.

She lay in an empty bed. Her thoughts and emotions were a crushing weight on her chest. She could barely breathe. She couldn't remember escaping that empty house, but she remembered standing in front of her husband's coffin. Then she heard Keller's voice, and turned to see him shamelessly standing there with his neatly-combed hair, blue suit, and calm, smug face.

The man thinks he's won. The thought came to her like icy steel. The hatred had seized her then.

It fueled her climb up the icy face. When Ruben next looked down at her, something in her stare gave him pause.

From above him, Raul glanced down. "What is it?"

Ruben returned to the task of climbing. "Nothing," he muttered.

III

Once they reached the next ledge, as before, Raul helped Ruben upward. The two of them pulled Anne up over the edge. A short span of ice wall stood in front of them. They climbed it to a lengthier, broader area of inclined ground.

Ruben stepped close to Anne. "Are you all right?" he asked her.

"No," she said, her eyes toward the snow of the ledge.

Ruben looked down. "I'm sorry. It's a bad question."

Anne raised her head and turned her eyes, sorrowful and tired, to Ruben. "It's all right, Ruben. I'm trying."

Raul studied the mountainside ahead. He nudged Ruben and pointed toward the top of the incline that supported them, where they saw a large vertical crack in the icy rock face.

"Shelter there," Raul said. He trudged upward toward it, and they followed.

The crevice opened into a cave. Numerous naturally-formed vertical furrows lined the interior walls, which glinted crystalline with ice.

It proved better inside the ice cave than outside

with the wind and snow. Ruben and Anne took refuge against the cave's left wall, sitting down. Anne's muscles felt like lead. She feared she might not be able to get up again.

Raul produced a small portable gas burner and began heating it. He packed glovefuls of snow into a round metal container and set it atop the burner. With no explanation offered, it soon became clear that Raul was melting the snow for water. Once done, he poured the liquid into small travel cups for them. They had a refreshing drink while Raul refilled the metal container with snow.

He produced a pouch of some pasty, chunky mixture. Once another batch of snow had melted, he mixed it with the water to create a sort of soup.

"Don't worry," Raul said with that smile he meant to be reassuring, but to Anne fell flat. "I will take good care of you." He returned his attention to the soup.

Anne wished for warmth. It had already been a long, difficult climb. The journey seemed as unlikely and impossible of a task as there might ever be. For all of her resolve, the sense of its possible futility kept returning to her.

She was paying Raul well, and Anne knew she would have to pay Ruben for his aid once this was over. Still, she couldn't imagine anyone would be so desperate for money to put themselves through this ordeal. With Ruben, at least, she knew it wasn't about money, even if he had mentioned it before. The man did have to make a living, as everyone did—everyone who hadn't been born into a lofty bank account like Keller. Fair payment for Ruben was the least she could do.

THE MOURNER'S CRADLE

Between shivers, with her hands bunched in her lap, she turned to Raul and asked, "How much longer until we get there?"

"There is still quite the climb," Raul responded, not what Anne wanted to hear, but she appreciated his frank honesty.

Anne struggled to remove her pack. Her hands and arms were stiff. Ruben saw her difficulty and moved to assist. Together, they pulled Anne's green supply pack free and set it aside.

Anne placed the duffel bag in her lap and unzipped it to reveal Damon's papers and the maps, including the patchwork map that Damon must have created during his last days. The camera hid somewhere beneath all of it.

She examined Damon's crude patchwork map and the marking across it, three X marks surrounding what Damon had believed to be the general location of what he had called the Mourner's Cradle. Even if her husband had drawn the map with a precise hand and a sharp mind, it struck her like something out of a child's pretend treasure hunting adventure.

She didn't know what substantiated Damon's fixation, but she knew Damon. Now that he was gone, his void was hers. For the moment, going over the patchwork map gave her something to do, a reason to move her hands, which she considered a good thing in this cold.

Raul glanced over, but quickly returned his eyes to the almost-finished soup.

Anne continued poring over the map. Still beside her, Ruben raised his head with a sudden motion. This drew Anne's attention. She laid her hands down against the map, crinkling the paper.

"What is it, Ruben?" she asked.

He didn't respond. He was listening. Raul looked up from the soup. He heard it also, as did Anne now. She sensed an unusual change in the cave's air. Penetrating the cave's silence, even through the wind outside, was a rhythmic, disquieting *crunch, crunch, crunch.*

FIRE IN THE NIGHT

I

Ruben began to rise. Raul held up a finger in caution.

"Wait here," he said. "I will look."

While Raul walked toward the mouth of the cave to investigate the sounds, Ruben came to his feet. Anne decided it wise to do the same. Her legs wobbled when she rose. Ruben put out an arm to steady her.

The crunching sounds had desisted. The heavy outside winds renewed their fury. Anne and Ruben watched Raul's dark form step into the light of the cave's opening.

In the middle of the cave, the soup bubbled.

The explosion sent Raul staggering backward. His body struck the cave floor. Blood streamed from the bullet hole in his forehead.

Anne cried out and rushed toward him. Ruben grabbed her arm to pull her back. She yanked away from Ruben but quickly understood he was right; Raul was already dead. Nothing could be done, and whoever had done this was *still out there*.

Hardly able to sort out what had happened, she forced her feet forward and rushed to the back of the cave. Ruben started to follow, but heard other footsteps in the same instant. The cave darkened as another figure stepped into the opening.

"I wouldn't move if I were you," a voice spoke. In the back of the cave, the cold feeling in Anne's veins turned to ice. She knew Keller's voice immediately.

"Put your hands up where we can see them," Keller said.

He moved aside for two more figures to appear at the cave's opening. One of the men held a black rifle, its sling dangling free. He trained the gun's sights on Ruben. Ruben raised both hands into the air.

It was the first time Ruben had ever seen Keller in anything other than the blue suit and tie he so often wore. Keller had geared up for the mountain, as had the other two, all bundled in thick, warm clothing tailored to defy the mountains' harsh freezing weather.

"Javier," Keller said, "if this man makes one wrong move, shoot him." Keller took a few slow steps forward and studied Ruben through the cave's dimness. "Ruben, is it?"

Ruben didn't reply.

"Yes, I'm sure of it," Keller said. "Ruben Ramirez. I remember you. You were an associate of Damon Sharpe's." Keller smacked his gloved hands together. "It's a small world sometimes, isn't it?"

The smile on Keller's lips evaporated. "It's too dark in here for my liking. Turn around slowly and come out of the cave, Mr. Ramirez. If you try anything, Javier here will gun you down without blinking twice. Hell, without blinking once, probably. Isn't that right, Javier?"

Javier kept his cold blue eyes on the sights and the

barrel pointed at Ruben's back. Ruben turned around to face them. He took in the other men for a moment of expressionless calculation before he started to walk.

"That goes for you, too, Miss—excuse me, *Mrs.*—Sharpe," Keller called toward the back of the cave.

They knew she was here. Trying to hide was pointless. Anne stepped out.

Javier kept the gun pointed at Ruben. The man's concentration didn't waver. Anne had a rather strong feeling that, if she made a move, Javier wouldn't hesitate to open fire.

She halted when she recognized the other man with Keller and Javier, the man who had attacked her in her own home.

"Oh, that's right," Keller said to Anne. "You and Vince have already met, haven't you? Wonderful. That will save us an introduction." He scanned the cave one last time and spotted the open duffel bag against one side of the cave. The corner of a sheaf of papers jutted out. Keller's eyes flicked to the heftier green supply packs before returning to the black-and-blue duffel bag.

"Is that what I suspect it is?" he asked.

"And what would that be?" Anne asked.

"Don't pretend to be stupid," Keller said. "I think you know why we've followed you here."

"No," said Anne, "but now I know you for the murdering piece of shit you are. I already knew you were a lying snake."

"Call me what you want, Mrs. Sharpe—"

"I will. Thanks."

Ignoring this, Keller resumed. "Damon Sharpe showed something to Cornwell that interested him, at least until I exposed your husband for the fraud he was."

"He was never a fraud," Anne said coldly, "despite what you may have told others."

"We'll find that out soon enough, won't we?" Keller replied. "That's part of the reason I'm here."

"I don't have any idea what you're talking about. All I know is that you've followed us to Peru, you just shot a man, and now you're pointing a gun at us."

"I never shot a man," Keller said. "That was Javier here. Make no mistake, he'll shoot you too, if you don't cooperate one-hundred-percent. First things first, Mrs. Sharpe—I can't help wondering about the possibility that there might have been something to this notion of your husband's, this Mourner's Cradle. You took the trouble to come this far, all the way to this hellish mountainside, and I'm thinking Cornwell would never have bought such a story without some solid assurance. Even if Cornwell isn't interested anymore, I am, and I'll find out what this is about before it's all over with. For now, I want both of you outside where I can keep an eye on you in the light. And pick up the bag, Mrs. Sharpe. I'll be interested in that, too."

She walked to the bag. Javier's rifle jerked toward her. She froze.

"Be careful, Mrs. Sharpe," Keller warned. Anne held up her hands and made a slow, deliberate motion to reach out and take the duffel bag by its strap. She lifted it.

"Now," Keller said, "both of you, outside."

Javier kept the rifle on Anne and Ruben. Keller walked toward the cave's exit. Vince, with an ugly

THE MOURNER'S CRADLE

lingering look toward Anne, turned to walk after Keller. Javier backed away, but the rifle's barrel never faltered. Ruben walked toward the light of the snow and the blinding outdoor sun. Anne followed. Raul's lifeless body lay motionless. The abandoned soup, still cooking, bubbled to the floor.

II

"I would like to know," Keller began, while Anne and Ruben stood on the white, slanted ground, "the exact reason why the two of you came here."

"You already know," Anne spoke, pushing each word from her lips as if spitting out a toxic chemical.

"I have a general idea, yes," Keller said, "but if I had the full story, I obviously wouldn't ask. Things might have gotten a bit out of control, I'll admit that, but your coming here gave me the perfect opportunity to correct our situation. You should have covered your tracks better, I might add, but apparently you didn't realize that I would go to these lengths to take what I want. But I always get what I want, and I don't think you'll doubt that again, not that you'll have the opportunity."

"Do you have a point?" Anne asked.

"Anne," Ruben uttered, keeping his voice low.

"As I said," Keller answered Anne. "Your husband must have been certain of something. Otherwise, you're just insane. You can set that bag down."

Anne dropped the bag. She kept her head upraised and her eyes on Keller, except when they shifted to where Vince stood leering at her from his position not far away. He wore bulkier layers and a black fur cap donned his bald head this time, but Anne had committed his unsightly features to memory.

He spoke with a frosty puff. "Remember me, bitch?"

"Yes, Vince, she remembers you," Keller said, suddenly sounding bored. "We've already established that."

"I ought to cut you up into little pieces," Vince said to Anne.

"Then grow a pair of balls and come over here and do it," Anne said right back.

Vince's eyes widened. Once he managed to process what she had said to him, he reached down to unzip a compartment of his jacket. He withdrew an object which Anne couldn't identify until the blade flicked out.

"I got no problem with that," Vince said, starting in her direction.

"Vince, don't be stupid," Keller said, stopping Vince in his steps. "Get back over here."

Javier aimed his rifle at Anne, but Anne's eyes held onto Vince.

"Go ahead, slink back to your boss like the lapdog you are," Anne said to him. "Your mouth is a lot bigger than your testicles, if you even have any."

Vince's eyes were like frozen stone. "We'll see," he said. He strode toward her.

"Vince," Keller said, louder this time. Vince ignored it. His switchblade was in his hand and he made no motions to put it away.

I'll cut this bitch open. That's what ran through his mind. Anne could see it in his face.

When he stepped close enough, she kicked snow at

him. It struck the front of his insulated legs. This was more than enough. Fury narrowed his eyes, his jaw clenched, and Vince came at her.

She ducked low. Vince tried to stop, or to grab at her, or both, but he didn't expect the sudden movement. He stumbled over her crouched form and fell into the snow. He braced himself against the snowy ground with one hand and struck out with the switchblade as Anne made a swift grab for it. The blade cut her glove and nicked her hand. Blood leaked into the small slit.

Vince cursed and stabbed again, but even at this close distance, his position was awkward and ineffective. Anne thrust her fingers at his eyes. Her effort fell short when something caught her arm, around her elbow; a strap, she thought. The strap of the duffel bag?

The distraction cost her a valuable second. Vince's free hand grabbed her wrist and twisted it. Anne clenched her teeth, her eyes watering with the pain. She rammed her head into his face.

Javier held his rifle poised for a shot, but he couldn't fire without hitting Vince. Vince and Anne slid in a flurry of snow dust. Both tumbled down the frozen slant. Keller backpedaled from their whirling path.

"Javier!" Keller shouted. "Shoot her!"

Javier fired. The bullet struck snow.

Anne and Vince struggled, grappling and rolling. Vince was gaining the upper hand for his raw strength. Anne thrust a knee upward for his groin, but Vince twisted to avoid this. Anne yanked the arm ensnared by the duffel bag's strap. The bag came between them as Vince thrust his knife at her and caught in the duffel bag. The bag ripped open. The knife spun away.

Keller kicked out when the two rolled past him. His boot struck something, but what, he wasn't sure. Before he could do much else, the two—oblivious to anything but their frantic fight to overcome the other—tumbled onto the portion of the incline that became a drastic downward slope.

"Vince!" Keller shouted. The two of them sailed down the slope toward the edge of the mountain ledge.

Ruben's heart pounded. He saw it happening and couldn't stop it, but he did realize Javier's rifle had strayed from him. He rushed at Javier.

Anne and Vince went over the edge. Javier heard the rapid steps, spun on Ruben, and fired. The rifle's blast reverberated across the icy mountain ledge. Ruben's vision filled with blood.

BLOOD ON THE SNOW

I

RUBEN KNEW IT was a desperate move, but alternatives were scarce. He had to do something.

To Ruben, everything slowed to a crawl. He leaned down to put his hand into the snow and curled his fist tight. When he came up, he ran, footsteps firing across the snow, and Javier turned the rifle on him.

Ruben hurled the ball of snow and ice. Fire sprang from the barrel of Javier's rifle and the snowball exploded into his face. Ruben dove, but not quickly enough.

The blast clipped him and red erupted through his vision. Warm wetness flooded the side of his face.

Carried by his momentum, Ruben crashed into Javier's legs. The rifle jerked. Javier slipped, flailing down the precarious slant and over the edge.

Ruben sprawled facedown into the snow. It reddened with his blood.

Keller stood in shock. He stood gaping at the white mountain ledge, at Ruben and the red snow around his head.

Keller made a crooked path toward the ice cave's opening. Outside it, he slumped against the cold mountain rock wall.

Anne Sharpe was dead. This he had no problem with. It would have been the end result anyway, but Keller hadn't been prepared for it to come in this fashion, at the cost of both Vince and Javier.

Javier, Keller couldn't care less about. He hadn't even met the man until recently, but Keller was sure that, once he got back to St. Charles, he would catch some heat about this incident. What could be done, though? Javier knew the risk. He took it every day in his line of work.

As for Vince, he shouldn't have fallen for Anne Sharpe's stupid little game, but the man didn't know any better and had died because of it.

Keller looked back to Ruben's still form and took a few deep breaths. Once he felt steady enough, he searched around for the duffel bag.

Where was it? He thought he remembered having Anne bring it out of the cave, but didn't see it anywhere around.

He walked over to Ruben's body, took him by a shoulder, and lifted him enough to look beneath. No, it wasn't there, either.

Where was it? Keller walked to where the incline dipped into the icy death-slide. He looked outward toward the end of the ledge where the drop-off had claimed Javier, Vince, and Anne Sharpe.

Surely it hadn't fallen off the mountainside? It didn't seem likely, but Keller didn't see it anywhere else even after another inspection.

A discrepancy in the glaring white snow caught his vision. Keller approached for a closer look, saw a piece of paper in the snow, and bent over to snatch it up.

It appeared to be a map with several strange

markings on it. He studied it and turned it to each side, trying to decipher what he was looking at. Was this one of Damon Sharpe's maps? It almost had to be, didn't it?

Anne and Ruben had died, to Keller's gratification. With any luck, he wouldn't have to worry about covering his tracks upon returning to St. Charles, except in the matter of Javier's death. He didn't relish the complications he expected to encounter over that situation.

It wasn't that alone which kept him on the snowy mountain, however. Something about this Mourner's Cradle had drawn him in, much like that plague of curiosity or obsession that had afflicted Damon and Anne Sharpe.

Keller smoothed his dark hair with a gloved hand. Looking over the map, he wandered into the ice cave.

||

Anne swung and kicked without thinking. Instinct and unthinking rage fueled every move. The force of Vince's fist glanced across her face, but she didn't relent. She battled until their momentum carried them down the slope of snow and ice and right over the edge.

She fought for reason in the rush of panic, wind, and snow below. She saw the white surface of the next ledge downward. It rushed toward her and toward Vince.

The duffel bag's strap still entangled her arm. She gripped it with both hands and bunched it beneath her with the last-minute thought that it could somehow soften the imminent impact.

Vince struck the white surface. Anne, duffel bag under her, crashed down on top of him. All thoughts she had managed to organize within the past seconds shattered from her grasp.

Black. White. Gray. White again.

Anne's eyes opened. At first, the bright white world blinded her. She struggled to stand, but collapsed into the snow.

She stared at the sky and blinked twice when the gunshot roared somewhere above.

Her dazed mind struggled to register what was happening. She strained to turn her head, but found it easier to move her eyes instead.

She sprawled on a ledge. A body was nearby—Vince's body, she remembered.

He didn't move. She had landed on top of him, she recalled. He had broken her fall, in part. The duffel bag, which had also assisted, lay torn open and half-buried in the snow.

A shout from above captured her sluggish senses. A dark figure catapulted down, struck the edge of the ledge where she and Vince lay, and bounced on downward, screaming over the side of the mountain.

It was Keller's other man, the one she hadn't recognized. She was fairly certain he wouldn't survive the fall.

It amazed Anne that she was still alive. She didn't know the extent of her injuries. She felt like death. She also felt like she was floating.

She tried to stand and managed to pull herself up to her knees before doubling over. Sickness and pain set in from all directions.

Anne attempted to crawl to the blue-black duffel

bag. She slumped two, three times into the snow, and struggled to pull herself together enough to move closer.

She reached for the bag and fell onto it. She laid her head on its surface.

Anne was nearer to Vince now. His chest was still. He had taken the worst of the fall and his neck was twisted at an unusual angle.

Anne couldn't seem to move her head from the bag that had become her pillow in the snow. Her eyes fell on the only thing she could discern from this point besides Vince's body, a sliver of landscape far below this mountain ledge.

The snow turned gray again. The colors of the world drained.

It's just as well that I die here, Anne mused. *I probably deserve it.* She had failed Damon and Ruben, about the only ones who mattered to her.

Anne fought to keep her eyes open against anything, but it proved too difficult. The gray world darkened. Her eyelids fell, and she dropped into sleep.

AWAKENING

I

IN A MOMENT of blurred consciousness, Ruben seized the pain and discomfort, awful as it was, and pushed against the beckoning sleep.

He raised his head from the snow and saw his own blood. He pressed a cold, shaking hand to his head, and felt wetness. He trembled when his fingers met the wound, rough and tender, and pain coursed through his senses.

He was lucky, in a manner. Although the injury was bloody, the shot had shaved away skin and nothing else.

He probed the site with his fingers. It made him gasp, but he had to verify his assessment of the injury.

It ran from the top of his cheek to his temple. It still bled. He pressed his hand against the open flesh to seal the wound. It burned with the pressure of skin against raw exposed meat. He winced. It hurt—a lot. He did his best to shake away his daze and tried to pull himself up.

He slid and struggled for traction. After almost a minute, he managed to climb to his feet. He backed away from the sharp slant that had delivered Javier over the mountain edge. *How long ago had that been?*

He looked toward the cave and around at the mountainside. He saw no one else around. What had happened to Keller?

Anne. Ruben swallowed. That was a much better question for now, he thought. Where was she? He felt a chilling answer rising from beneath his dread.

With a moment's hesitation, he crept toward the edge where Anne and Vince had gone over, followed by Javier during Ruben's last moments of consciousness. He took special care with his steps. He didn't want to share the same end.

A freezing gust swept across him. He shivered and clenched his teeth to keep them from chattering.

Anne was probably dead. Ruben couldn't keep denying that likelihood to himself, but if there was any chance, any possibility in the world that she might be alive . . .

He dug into the snow to maintain the securest grip possible. Inching forward, he peered over the edge. He saw Vince's body lying near the brink of the ledge below. Closer to the mountain wall, he could see Anne. She wasn't moving.

He feared the worst, but leaving her wasn't an option. He had to climb down.

He still felt woozy and couldn't refrain from touching the bloody side of his head again. The wound needed tending. There were supplies back in that cave, bandages included.

Ruben rose, facing the edge, and backed away with slow steps. He moved toward the cave, and stopped when he saw Raul's body on the ground. After a moment, he took a deep breath and pressed on. Though it stirred awful feelings in him, he could do nothing for the man.

When Ruben made it to the cave's opening, he stopped again, feeling dizzy. He rested against the wall. When the odd sensation dissipated, he thought again about Javier's fall. He wondered about Keller.

Ruben didn't have a direct answer, but he recognized the possibility that Keller was still around somewhere. He glanced around but saw no potential weapon, not even a rock, that he could use for self-defense.

He stood up straight, took his hand from the icy wall, and walked into the cave. Halfway through, he saw the supply packs. He approached and reached down to open one of them.

He paused. Had he heard something? He listened, but his ears could pinpoint nothing aside from the outside whistling wind.

It was a trick of the wind or of the mind, he guessed. He mentally berated himself for wasting time and opened the supply pack. He sifted through the contents until he found a roll of bandages and a tube of ointment. He opened the tube and smeared the ointment across his injury, though it stung, and applied a quick bandage-job to his head. This would have to do for now.

When he returned to the ledge, he put his full weight into each step, allowing his boots to sink into the snow and the crampons' spikes to grip the ice beneath. He slammed an ice axe into the ground where the steep decline reached its worst point.

He sank to one knee, then the other. He lowered a

leg over the vertical ice wall and searched for a foothold. It took minutes before he found one, and barely a stable one at that. He dug in hard and tried to lower himself while gripping the handle of the axe.

Ruben was no expert climber in this icy environment, but Raul was no longer here to advise or assist him in his efforts. He depended on his own lackluster skills and a sense of desperation. He clung to the white face and started a gradual descent. Now was the time for care, not for fear. Even with the wind picking up, Ruben thought he could hear his own heart pounding like a drum to precede a military-style execution.

He swallowed and pulled the axe free from the ice. He swung it against a lower section of ice a few times until it broke through. Once he gained a better hold, he lowered himself another step. When he found the next foothold, he dug his boot in and tested it before putting his weight into another downward step.

The rest of the descent was equally nerve-wracking. It seemed to Ruben that he was a second away from losing control. Just when he wondered if he would ever reach the ground of the next ledge down, his foot touched a semi-solid surface below.

With a glance down, he saw he had reached the ground. Nearby lay Anne. Farther away, next to the edge of the subsequent drop-off, was Vince.

||

"Anne."

She heard his voice but assumed it had to be death's delirium teasing her one final time.

"Anne!" Ruben's voice became more insistent. He shook her by the shoulder. She opened her frosty eyes to glare, or attempt to glare since the cold sleep dulled her senses and she could only muster a spoonful of anger now.

Everything was blurred. She blinked several times before she could make out his features. She studied his face and his dark hair blowing in the wind. His eyes, appearing almost black, looked down at her.

"Ruben," she said. She tried to shake her head against the snow. "It's over."

"No," Ruben said. "Get up, Anne."

"I can't get up." His suggestion seemed outrageous.

Ruben pulled back the fabric of her clothing where he could, examining her skin in multiple areas. The sudden intrusiveness of the act kindled a frozen anger in her. Her hand clenched into a fist.

"Ruben, stop," she whispered through clenched teeth.

"I have to make sure your bones aren't broken," he said. "Hold still."

Despite his telling her to hold still, she grappled for every ounce of movement she could regain. Ruben now seemed agitated. They both were, but for now, as impossible as it had seemed not long ago, they were alive.

Ruben located a bruise on Anne's ribs. When he touched it, she gasped. She tried to pull away. He withdrew, but leaned close and touched the bruise more gently. It was yellow around its edges with a splotch of dark brown in the middle—not too bad, given what he had expected.

He pulled the layers of cloth upward. "Ruben," Anne said. "You can leave my clothes on, thanks."

"I'm trying to help you," Ruben said. "Is that a problem?"

"If Damon was still here, he might throw you off the side of this mountain, you know."

"Would he?" Ruben asked. "I don't think I ever even saw him step on an insect."

"Remember when I left my job?" she asked. Ruben gave her a quizzical glance.

"The secretary job?"

"Office assistant."

"I think so," he said. "That was a long time ago."

As he spoke, Ruben kept pushing and prodding. When he reached a tender area, she drew in a sharp breath and expelled it in a fierce sigh. She followed this with a stare as cold as the ice that surrounded them both.

"It was a shit job," Anne resumed, "but back in those days, I did what I had to do to help make ends meet. My last day—"

Anne fell into a round of coughing before she managed to continue. "My boss was a real jerk. One day, he said the wrong thing to me. I don't even remember what it was now. I went home and told Damon about the disrespect he had been heaping on me for months."

She stopped as if about to start coughing again, but didn't. Instead, the twitch of a smile came to her lips. "I might have exaggerated about it. Just a bit. Damon didn't say much at the time, but do you know what he did? He came out to see me, and when my boss walked in and opened his mouth to harass me for talking instead of working, Damon punched him. Knocked him out with one punch.

"As you might guess, that was my last day at work.

I couldn't find work again after that, so I mostly stayed home to take care of things while Damon was busy. It was hard sometimes to make things work, but I always appreciated what Damon did for me, even if it wasn't characteristic of who other people thought he was, even if it wasn't the smartest thing he could have done in our situation. I'll always remember the shocked look on that idiot's face the second Damon's fist smashed into it." Her faint sardonic smile was slow to fade. "Ruben, are you almost done?"

"I'm done." Ruben had been listening to Anne even if he was still checking her throughout it, but her health was of the foremost concern. She was battered and he first thought she might have some broken ribs. After a careful inspection, he couldn't affirm this was the case. He hoped it wasn't.

Vince's fall had seen a different outcome. At a glance, the man's injuries appeared far more severe. Of course, he was dead, so that went without saying.

Anne's senses were sharpening, Ruben judged. She had regained some humor also, even if not the sort that suited Ruben's tastes.

"You'll live," Ruben said to her. "I think, and I'm sure you'll agree, that it's time we make a decision. Where should we go from here?"

Anne looked at him for several seconds before responding, "Upward."

"Seriously?"

"Seriously."

"I said you would live. I didn't say you were in any shape to climb up the mountain."

"I'll try." She shifted, struggled, and fell still. "Since when are you a doctor, anyway?"

"I've done my studies."

"So? I've read a few murder mysteries, but that doesn't make me a detective. You're going to have to help me up."

"You had trouble the first time," Ruben said. "You're going to keep trying to move around in your condition? That isn't smart."

Anne leveled a gaze at Ruben which suggested he probably shouldn't say that again. She wasn't smiling.

"Help me up, Ruben," she said at length.

Ruben moved over to her. He slid his arms underneath her back and shoulders and pulled her upward. She grimaced. A soft gasp escaped her.

"All right, Ruben, put me back down," she said in a hurry, and he released her. She relaxed into the snow, panting for breath.

III

It took several more efforts, but Anne was persistent. Ruben complied each time until she was at last able to sit up. She leaned against him.

"If we go up," Ruben said to her, making certain she knew full-well what could happen, "we might not survive this."

"Speak for yourself."

"I'm speaking for both of us because I know it's the truth. We'll either freeze to death or our injuries will get the best of us."

Anne's head came up as something occurred to her. "What happened to Keller?"

Ruben shook his head.

"He's dead?"

"I don't know," Ruben said.

Anne looked away as the incessant wind struck her face. She looked over the edge of the ledge that supported them and into the distance, down to the white that enveloped the rocky terrain far below.

"I hope he isn't still out there," she said, "alive."

Ruben was silent. He had already acknowledged that possibility, but the immediate situation was more important. He looked up to the icy face that would take them, if they were able to conquer it, to the ledge where they found their previous resting spot in the mountainside cave.

If they could make it back there, where shelter and their supplies waited for them, they might have a chance. They could recover. They could eat and, if Raul's burner still worked, they could melt snow for water.

"If we are going to try to climb back up, we shouldn't wait any longer," Ruben said.

Anne responded by struggling to pull her legs up. A wave of pain and weariness stanched her efforts.

Ruben caught her, his arm around her shoulders. He rose slowly, trying to keep her steady and pull her upward along with him. The majority of the effort was Ruben's, but soon Anne was on her feet. She clung to him for support. Ruben shuffled forward, keeping her against the icy wall.

"Wait here," he said, and left. She managed to maintain her weight against the wall while Ruben stepped over to Vince's body.

He noticed Vince's supply pack beside him. It held on by one remaining strap. Ruben pulled it away from the dead man, knowing it might well be loaded with survival necessities including food in some form, and slung it over his shoulder. He also spotted the duffel bag in the snow and retrieved it before returning to Anne.

She still braced herself against the mountainside. The wind calmed down now. Ruben and Anne stood in quiet for almost a minute and surveyed the obstacle before them. Their exhalations hissed white in the cold. Anne lowered her head.

"I'm ready," she said at last, and met Ruben's gaze.

Ruben shoved his ice axe under an arm and checked his climbing gear. After this, he worked on securing Anne's.

"Ruben?" Anne spoke. From the snowy ground at her feet where Ruben straightened the crampons on Anne's climbing boots, he looked up to her.

"Please don't let me fall," she said.

THE ICE CAVE

I

THE CLIMB WAS agonizing. It required every bit of Ruben's strength and attention to keep Anne from falling. As for Ruben, he felt faint again, a likely combination of his head wound, the rigors of their ordeal, and nature's frigid indifference.

He almost lost his grip several times and came dangerously close to tumbling down from the wall, taking Anne with him. Throughout the climb, Ruben kept her near to make certain that, if anything disastrous did happen, he could make a last-ditch effort to save her.

The climb was as torturous as both of them had imagined it might be and then some. It seemed endless.

Ruben supported Anne with one arm when she needed to stop, but it put a horrible strain on him. It left him with one arm to cling to the ice, doing his best to hold on while digging in his feet and hoping the supporting ice wouldn't break apart.

Anne's mind swirled. What little strength she retained ebbed, and weakness threatened to take her down. She was slowing again, but if she let go, it would be over.

Ruben looked over to lend quiet reassurance. "Almost there," he said.

Anne saw this was true. It strengthened some vestige of her resolve. She heaved ever upward, and Ruben continued to climb with her though the awkward ascent became no easier.

"Keep going," Ruben urged in a whisper. "We're almost there."

"I'm trying!" Anne hissed. She felt a sudden compulsion to smack him off of the mountain wall. Instead, she gritted her teeth and fought to climb. The surge of anger ignited her resolve. When she peeked over the top of the wall, the anger began to seep away. For the first time since she could remember, she felt a trace of hopefulness. It bolstered her last efforts to pull herself over the edge.

She crawled back onto the upper plateau and collapsed into the snow. The ground's slant was precarious here, but she didn't think she could move any farther after the intense exertion. Then again, she hadn't expected to endure it in the first place.

Ruben climbed up and over to join her. "Anne," he said. She ignored it, but he started prodding her. She stirred, but that was it. Ruben expelled a heavy sigh and leaned to situate an arm beneath her. He used his other arm to steady himself against the steeply-sloped surface. He slogged upward and heaved against his own exhaustion to drag Anne up the snowy incline.

He stopped several times. Each time, he took slow, deep breaths to stabilize his oxygen and rubbed his hands against his thighs before resuming. After a few minutes, he made it halfway up the slope. It took several more minutes to reach more stable ground, where the task became easier and he could use both arms to drag her the rest of the distance.

Anne felt the cold recede a small amount and noticed the relenting of the winds. She opened her eyes, blinking, to absorb the welcome sight of their shelter.

Ruben fell against a wall of the ice cave. He caught his breath and made a mental effort to reorient himself before he deposited the bags from his shoulder to the ground. He opened one of the supply packs, pulled out what blanketing he could find, and set to wrapping Anne as snugly as possible.

She might have thanked him, but felt too tired for words and instead gave him a slow blink before she closed her eyes again.

Ruben spotted the gas burner in the middle of the cave. It had gone out. The ruined soup-mixture splattered the ground around it. Ruben fetched the burner and set it against one side of the cave.

It helped that the interior of the cave was slightly warmer than outside, but the warmth of the blankets seemed scarce. Ruben applied himself to building a modest flame.

He felt exhausted, but the warmth helped. He touched the bandage around his head. The injury remained sore, but it appeared he would survive for now, as would Anne.

An insistence prodded into the back of his thoughts, another thought of Keller. What had happened to him? Was he dead after their conflict? Was he still out there on the snowy mountainside?

He had no answers for any of this, but for these doubts Ruben decided at least one of them should try to stay alert. He bundled himself with the remaining blankets and laid back against a wall of the ice cave to rest, but did not sleep.

II

The day darkened. Anne slept long, and it became difficult for Ruben to remain awake into the later hours. He climbed to his feet to find his arms and legs uncomfortable and stiff. It would do some good for him to move around, he decided. He sorted through the packs to find some provisions. With a shock, he noticed one of the supply packs was missing.

This could only mean one thing. *Keller had been here.*

A dull alarm bleated in the back of Ruben's mind. He acknowledged it but continued about the business of finding food.

At least he had managed to retrieve Vince's pack from the lower ledge. It wasn't much, but it did contain some food. They needed anything they could find. Raul's pack was also here. Inside it, Ruben found one of the pouches of paste-like substance that looked much like what Raul had used to make soup.

He examined the pouch, thinking he wasn't quite brimming with energy now and didn't feel like tinkering with the gas burner any more than necessary. He just wanted something to sustain himself and Anne.

He went into the packs again and found a few other items which included some bags of dried fruit, salted nuts, and a pack of crackers that had been reduced to powder. These were all edibles which he wouldn't have to thaw or cook, so this was dinner.

He gave Anne a gentle shake. "Anne," he said.

She didn't respond. He shook her again. "Anne," he repeated.

She opened her eyes, confused for a couple of seconds before she focused on Ruben.

"What?" she asked.

"We need to eat," he said. He held out a plastic bag of dried orange, apple, and banana pieces. He tilted another smaller bag of mixed nuts into it and allowed the larger half to slide down into the fruit bag, which he waved in front of her.

"Here," he said.

It took a moment for her to work her arm out of the blanket wrap and accept the food. She tried to sit up, but failed. Ruben put a hand on her arm.

"There's no need to get up," he said. "I'll get you something to drink."

Once Ruben said this, he wished he hadn't. It meant he would have to try getting the gas burner started after all. It was their only means of melting the snow for decent drinking water.

First, he found, the burner had exhausted its fuel supply. He located a tin of fuel in one of the bags and refilled it. To his relief, after cleaning off what he could of the overcooked brown crust of soup caked to it, he found it operable.

He soon had the burner working again, with a snow-packed cup resting on it. Before much longer, he had the water ready.

Ruben held the metal cup up to her. Anne roused herself to take it. She worked her arms back out of the blanket and frowned at their soreness, but accepted the cup from Ruben. Though an uncomfortable effort, she could readjust herself to a better angle for drinking her water. She sipped at it as the two ate a quiet, somber meal of dried fruit, nuts, and cracker-dust.

Afterward, they didn't speak much. Anne couldn't stave away the sleep. Ruben tried to stay awake, but his own exhaustion became heavier. He dropped against the wall of the cave again, slouched, and bundled himself in the closest warming articles he could find.

Thoughts of warning bounced in his mind, but despite them, he just couldn't stay awake.

Hours later, Anne woke again. She shifted within her blanket cocoon and tried to look around. Her neck hurt. The more she tried to move, the worse she felt. She decided to relax instead.

"Ruben?" she whispered. No answer came. Anne looked toward the mouth of the cave. Through it, she could see only snow.

She didn't bother with Ruben a second time. He was out, not that she could blame him. He had been through a lot himself, but the both of them still had so much farther to go.

Anne could do little until she built up her strength, she acknowledged, but she couldn't help wanting to look at that patchwork map of Damon's. It was in the duffel bag, wasn't it? She supposed Ruben had brought it up with the other supplies, unless she had carried it up herself without realizing. She doubted that, but she couldn't really remember.

She didn't want to get up now, though, as cold as she was even while wrapped in her sleeping bag and blankets. She wished Ruben could retrieve it for her.

She needed to be patient, she told herself, even if she didn't want to be.

Anne remained awake for many more minutes, thinking, and the time dripped into a half-hour or more before a random crunch alerted her. She turned her head against the shock of pain jolting through her neck, but she saw only Ruben. He had climbed back to his feet and ambled across the cave to check on her.

"Anne? Are you all right?"

"What do you think?"

"Is there anything I can do?"

"No, Ruben. Not really. But thank you."

Ruben, gloved hands in the front pockets of his coat, nodded and returned to the burner. Anne heard a bubbling a short time after. Ruben had started the burner.

In another few minutes, the rich aroma of coffee reached Anne's senses. She inhaled it deeply. The coffee smelled, and sounded, wonderful.

III

Anne knew she had to try getting up and moving around if she wanted to make a suitable recovery. It would be as necessary to move as it would be to eat and drink. The remaining supplies would only last so long, especially considering the matter of the return trip, which she hadn't even thought about until now.

She had a lot to think about. It seemed surreal that she had been so close to death. She was still trying to process Keller's sudden appearance here and the attempt on her and Ruben's lives. Keller was a snake in more than one manner.

Ruben's voice interrupted her thoughts. "How are you feeling?" he asked, watching Anne limp around the cave until she had to stop to lean against one of its walls.

"Better," she said.

Ruben started some more coffee. Before long they had their meal from an unmarked pouch of dried poultry-substance found in Vince's bag and drank more of the warm coffee that seemed a luxury to them now.

On her continued walk around the cave, Anne encountered the blue-and-black duffel bag. She dug through the papers inside it for the patchwork map. Her initial quick search came up empty. She pulled all of the papers out, ruffling through them again and afterward stacking them on the floor of the ice cave. Still she saw no sign of the patchwork map.

"What the hell?" she murmured. Where was it?

She looked into the empty bag and saw the light peeking through a rip in its bottom. Bunched into one corner of the bag was the camera, which the bag had somehow retained, but the patchwork map was gone along with her wedding ring, no doubt lying lost in the snow somewhere down the horrid cliffs of this massive mountain.

She felt sick. She had to sit down.

"What's wrong?" Ruben asked. Anne shook her head and raised a hand to her temple. She ran her fingers through her hair. Ruben continued to watch her. She didn't speak for some time. As Ruben looked away to the cave's opening, Anne swallowed, forced the image of that tarnished circle of gold and its cold diamond to the back of her mind, and thought again of the patchwork map.

"Do we still have Raul's map of the area?" she asked Ruben.

He walked to where the supply packs sat against the cave wall and went through Raul's pack until he found a white folded piece of paper. He opened it, peered at it, and passed it to Anne. She dropped it into her lap and placed her shiny cup of coffee on the ground beside her.

It took a few minutes of sitting there with Raul's map before her, analyzing it, thinking, pushing away the distractions, before her memory began to retrieve details of the map she had studied countless times before. Her mind had been awry since her fall over the ledge, but somewhere within, the image was there. In part, she could recall her husband's crudely-sketched work.

She tried to envision the patchwork map of the mountainside region where Damon had theorized the Mourner's Cradle to be. Three X's were marked at equal distances from one another, along with a question mark in their center.

What else? She kept searching, trying to remember and reconstruct the mental puzzle.

Over the minutes, the map in her mind came into clearer focus. She hoped her memory was accurate. The thought of climbing back down the mountain to search for the map that might have fluttered out was appalling. It wasn't going to happen at this stage.

Ruben saw her studying Raul's map. He took a sip of his coffee, which was growing cold, and glanced around the cave.

"Does this mean you're ready to start climbing again?" he asked.

"I'm not sure I am," Anne said, "but whether I'm ready or not, we'll have to." She raised her eyes to him. "Damon's map is gone."

"What?" Ruben asked, half-alarmed.

"It's fine," Anne said. "I had the map almost memorized, really, and now I'm doing my best to recall what I can. We have Raul's map right here. I think we can still get to where we need to be."

"Are you sure?"

"No, Ruben, I'm not, but it's all I have."

Ruben returned to drinking his coffee in silence.

"From everything I can remember about the map," Anne said, "and I think I can even remember Damon saying something about this once, there are supposed to be three indicators that might have surrounded the Mourner's Cradle at one point in time. What they could be, or how Damon came by this information, I have no idea, and we don't know whether anything like that is even still there."

"You're right," Ruben said. "We don't know that any of it will still be there."

Anne raised her head again. She sensed something more to Ruben's words.

"We're lucky we aren't dead after what happened to us," Ruben said, "and we don't know what's going to be up there or if we will even find the right location."

"What are you saying, Ruben?"

Ruben wiped his nose with a sleeve.

"I know you want to finish what Damon started," he said. "I respected his work more than almost anyone, but this—I don't know, Anne. Any findings, no matter how small, would be great, but what if there is nothing up there?"

Anne abruptly looked away from him.

"Anne," Ruben said. "I'm sorry. I'm just trying to help you understand our situation as I see it. What we're doing isn't reasonable. We have our lives. Why don't we go back while we can? While we're still able?"

Anne stared toward the cave wall. When she turned her head forward again, it remained tilted downward. When she raised her head, Ruben could see the tears in her eyes.

"How could you say that to me?" she asked.

"I'm sorry."

"Do you want to leave me now?" she asked. "Turn your back on me? Leave me alone up here?"

Ruben started to take another drink of coffee, but saw that his cup was empty. He gazed down into the cup.

"No," he said.

"Then do us both a favor, Ruben," she said, "and don't ever say anything like that to me again."

IV

By the following morning, Anne's health had improved even more. By contrast, Ruben's nose was running and he felt a bit under-the-weather. He muttered as much but didn't receive an answer. Anne's determination had returned in full, more so than ever before.

They opened another of Vince's pouches, which contained a portion of salted pork. Anne wasn't delighted with the selection, but food was food. Ruben brewed a beverage using melted snow and a packet of some frozen fruit mixture—cranberry, they soon discovered. All of this they downed with the last of the cracker crumbs. Afterward, Anne tried her steps around the cave again while Ruben started coffee. Almost half of a tin of gas remained for the burner.

Despite his touch of illness, Ruben did at least feel more optimistic about this day. Anne felt better, too. In their separate ways, both hoped things would go well, but when they started climbing again, anything could happen.

Anne ventured out of the cave, but not for long. The outside elements didn't daunt her, but she knew she should conserve her recovered strength for what lay ahead.

Ruben changed the bandage on his head. He smeared more of the ointment into the wound, which looked better than before, and rewrapped it with a clean white bandage.

When the coffee was done, Ruben poured each of them a steamy cup. The two of them sat down near a wall of the cave to drink their black coffee.

"This is it?" Ruben asked her. "Onward? Upward?"

"That's the gist of it," Anne said.

"I can't believe you got me into this," he said.

"You could have said no," she replied. Ruben mulled this and nodded. He returned to his coffee.

She touched his arm, leaning closer. "But I'm glad you didn't," she added quietly.

After they finished their coffee, Ruben gathered everything they would need for the rest of the journey: their climbing equipment and provisions, plus any extra provisions he could find in Vince's bag. Anne handed him the camera.

"Be careful with this, please," she said. He transferred it into one of the packs with care.

As Ruben worked, he wondered for an instant what had ever happened to Javier's bag. It must have sailed down the mountainside with him, he decided, and perhaps there wasn't any use in thinking any more about it.

A thought of Keller lurked in the back of his mind.

Ruben packed away the sleeping bags and blankets. He transferred the portable gas burner into his own supply pack along with its half-tin of fuel. Last, he jammed Vince's remaining food items into his and Anne's supply packs. He had some difficulty sealing the bulging packs shut, but prevailed.

Anne was already gearing up. Ruben did the same, and once he finished, he saw she stood watching him.

"Are you ready?" she asked.

Not long ago, he wouldn't have imagined her asking such a question. She had made a remarkable recovery, Ruben thought, though he suspected her condition must be worse than she was willing to admit or display in front of him.

Either way, she was ready, and right now she looked at him, waiting. He gave her a nod. It was time to face the mountain again.

UPWARD

I

ANNE SOON DISCOVERED she hadn't regained as much strength as she thought. Pushing herself up the powdery incline was an awful affair. She fought to cling to the sharply-slanted surface of the mountain while the snow kept giving away beneath her feet. She saw solid ground not far below, but as she climbed, this changed. The ground became more distant and deadly. She kept her eyes in front of her and above, where Ruben climbed ahead.

"Take your time," Ruben had said to Anne before beginning this newest ascent. "Don't take any chances. We need to take it slow and steady. Just be careful. If you fall behind, I can wait."

True to Ruben's indication, it hadn't taken long for Anne to fall behind. Ruben strained to maintain his hold on the mountainside. He knew Anne must be struggling all the more.

Anne forced herself upward. Ruben, watching her below, pushed himself to do the same. Throughout the slow, hard climb, distractions peppered their thoughts.

Ruben remembered that Anne had agreed to pay him for this. The thought almost made him laugh through his teeth. Money meant nothing up here among these icy rocks so far from the civilized world.

Ruben hadn't hurled himself into this horrid trial for money. He had no family. Anne didn't either, anymore. She didn't have much left in this world. She had Ruben and she had this outlandish desire of fulfilling Damon's unseen obsession, finding the Mourner's Cradle if anything existed of it.

Ruben and Anne both had their reasons for pushing on, even if neither fully realized them by this point. They just kept climbing. To stop would mean death.

To Anne, turning away now was inconceivable. She meant to continue against all odds. Much had been sacrificed and it wasn't over yet. From all she could recall of Damon's patchwork map, an answer awaited them some short distance beneath the mountain's summit.

How much longer? When would it end? Anne longed for a cup of Ruben's warm coffee or anything that would warm her, but they couldn't stop now.

Ruben hadn't spoken much since they left the ice cave, now far behind them. Not only was he saying almost nothing, he slowed in his climb. This did make it easier for Anne to keep up.

Thoughts like this, small details, turned in Anne's mind as they ascended the icy face.

||

When they reached the next slant that would support them, Ruben stopped. Gravity was no ally here, but this appeared to be the best they would find for some distance.

"I'm sorry," Ruben said, "but I have to rest." He touched the bandage on his head.

"Are you all right?" Anne asked.

"I'm just not feeling good. I keep feeling dizzy. Can we rest?"

She nodded. "It's cold, though. We don't have a shelter here."

"We have that," he said with a gesture toward an overhanging formation of rock.

"That isn't much of anything."

"We can try to dig a shelter beneath it."

"Dig?"

Without answering, Ruben took out his ice axe. Anne watched, dubious, as he moved forward and swung it into the snow to dislodge a portion. After a minute, Anne took out her own axe and came in to assist. She was careful to give Ruben plenty of space.

"How deep should we make this?" she asked.

"We shouldn't dig for long," Ruben said. "We only need enough room to burrow ourselves in. Our body heat will do the rest to keep us warm. It's the best we can do up here."

Anne wanted to continue climbing. She wasn't tired, but she didn't want to push Ruben. She could tell he didn't feel up to speed, although she hadn't aired these thoughts. Before, Ruben had pushed the concern of his head injury aside for her sake. It might be catching up with him. Prolonged exposure to the freezing elements couldn't be helping the situation.

The sharp cracking of Ruben's axe into the ice roused Anne from her ruminations. She rejoined him in digging the sub-shelter.

Ruben stopped and wiped his forehead with a

sleeve. Anne looked down at the rough basin they had cleared. "Do you think that's enough?" she asked.

"It will have to be," Ruben said.

They dug themselves into the hole. Anne found it miserable. She supposed the circulation of body heat Ruben referred to would take some time to accumulate. She couldn't sleep, but Ruben had no problem nodding away within minutes.

They rested against one another. Anne remained awake. She wished Ruben would wake up. She felt the urge to talk. She couldn't stanch the bombardment of her own thoughts.

It wasn't only the shock of the disastrous encounter with Keller and the others. Though that memory remained prominent, as did the brutal scene of Raul's sudden death, the coldness and the more immediate concerns served to distance her from the occurrence as if it had happened long ago.

She thought of the morning when she had found Damon cold and pale in their bed, and her mind shifted to the previous night when everything had been so different.

Damon sat in his makeshift study, surrounded by stacks of information. He read through the books around him and took up his black ballpoint pen every so often to write. Anne had slipped in to wish him goodnight, initially, but hadn't said anything in the end. He had paused in his writing to accept the drink from her. They shared their last moment without words.

Damon came to bed late. He never woke up again.

Now Anne was here, buried almost halfway into the frozen white snow of the mountain. What really brought her here? Was it madness or passion?

Passion? She almost laughed. It was Damon's passion, not hers, and this was Anne's futile attempt to salvage it from the grave.

Damon's passion, one component that drew her to him, had always intrigued her. She had never been particularly passionate about anything.

She would never have guessed it on the first day she met him at that cheerless party—one of Tabby Reinhart's gatherings, she recalled.

Tabby had always been decent enough, Anne supposed, but she could do without the rest of them. She remembered walking around with a wine spritzer in her hand, forcing small conversation with people she either didn't know or didn't care to speak to. After an insipid quarter-of-an-hour, she gave up and excused herself to step outside.

There she saw him. He sat outside, alone, on the ground with his back against the front of the red brick house. Cradled between his legs was an open bottle of scotch. An empty glass sat on the ground next to him.

"Not to piss on anybody's parade," the young, brown-haired man said without looking to see who had come out, "but this party is for the birds."

At least someone finally said it, Anne remembered thinking. Damon turned his head and seemed surprised, as if he had expected someone else. He offered her a drink. She gave it a thought, but declined. He poured himself another glass, set the bottle back in its place, and leaned back against the wall.

She felt more comfortable outside, in his company, than she had inside where the rest stirred their drinks and made small talk. Before the night ended, Damon asked Anne if she wanted to go for a walk.

"Sure, let's go," she responded.

Their walk took them from the spacious, well-lit brick house near the corner, through the open gate of its property, and down the dark street, where they cut across the next street and walked along its opposite side. Anne gave Damon a questioning glance. He didn't seem to notice.

It wasn't the best neighborhood, but she allowed Damon to lead her. She didn't know why. She didn't ask. She couldn't resist a quiet laugh.

He turned back toward her. "What?" he asked.

"I don't even know your name," she said.

"Sorry about that," he said, and stopped. "I'm Damon. Damon Sharpe."

"Anne Moore," she responded, and the two resumed their walk.

Along the dark, empty street, they walked and talked until, to their mild surprise, they neared that stretch leading toward the long row of hedges bordering Summerset Park, and just before it, that narrow road curving toward Marion Cemetery.

Now that she thought about it again these years later, Anne could hardly believe they had walked so far.

Even on that night of years ago, a man advanced in many years, a whispering man wearing a ruby ring, wandered the cemetery. His whispers carried on the breeze of the late hour, though Anne scarcely heard the sound and never knew its source.

The thought of the cemetery and an unmarked grave somewhere among its stones, Damon's grave, broke through Anne's memory and a stark coldness swept the streets of St. Charles into the past.

III

At the sound of Ruben's moan, Anne parted from her dozing memories. She readjusted herself in the cold orifice that housed their bodies and pulled an arm free. She tugged one of her gloves loose and reached out to touch the side of Ruben's face. The warmth startled her.

She considered waking him to ask how he felt, but decided against it. He needed the rest. It couldn't be easy to sleep up here, she guessed. She nestled against him and hoped the warmth of her body would help him against the cold. She had to do whatever she could.

Another moan left him. She glanced back to him. His eyes blinked open.

"Anne?" he whispered.

"Ruben," she answered in as reassuring of a voice as she could summon. "How are you feeling?"

He shook his head. He appeared bewildered. He tried to twist his body around inside the small niche.

"Just try to rest," Anne urged him. He stopped in his movements, looked past her for an instant, and relaxed. He still seemed half-asleep.

He gazed past her again, and his eyes sharpened. She had the sudden suspicion that sleep wasn't in the cards. Ruben began struggling to pull himself out of the hole. Anne sighed with annoyance.

"Ruben, what is it?" she asked.

He muttered something she couldn't understand. He placed both gloved hands on the snowy ground, heaving to wiggle his body free.

"What is so important?" Anne asked him. "Do you have to use the bathroom or something?"

After the word "bathroom" left her mouth, its ridiculousness struck her. A bathroom, up here?

"No," Ruben said. Now free, he planted both boots on the snowy mountainside. From the edge of his tone, he was more well-awake than she had thought.

"I saw him," he said. He pointed up the mountain. "Up there!" He started in that direction.

"Who?" Anne asked, rather confused.

"Keller!"

"What? Are you serious?"

Ruben whirled back toward her. "Would I lie?"

"Well, no, I guess not."

Anne climbed out of the hole with visibly more ease than Ruben. Her eyes searched the white-coated mountain rocks ahead and higher above, where Ruben had gestured. She couldn't see a thing aside from rocks and snow.

Ruben's steps met increasing difficulty. He almost slid in his attempts to hasten up the snowy ground. He stopped before reaching the vertical climb that would make their continued journey more difficult, and looked to the higher outcropping of rocks above.

In no hurry, Anne walked to join him. When she stepped up beside him, he shook his head and continued scanning the rocks along the upper plateau.

"Are you sure you saw him?" Anne asked.

He sighed a frosty-white breath and touched the bandage again. He wiped his nose with the opposite sleeve.

"No," he said. "I thought I saw something, and I thought it was him. Now I don't see anything." He studied the cluster of rocks one more time, stepped back, and rubbed the top of his head.

"Maybe you're right," he said. "I should probably try to rest before we continue the climb. I just don't know whether I'll be able to sleep now."

"We can do whatever you feel up to doing," Anne said, "but you don't seem that well to me."

Ruben didn't argue with her. He came back down to the opening they had dug.

"I'm fine, really," he said. "But thank you." He climbed down into the small hole. She rejoined him for the sake of warmth. Pushing back into the crude, narrow opening presented more of a pain than she remembered.

She thought about the gas burner and considered starting it to heat some soup or melt some water, but she couldn't recall where it was and didn't feel like digging through their packs for an eternity to find it.

Ruben rested. Though his eyes and mouth were closed, the muscles in his jaw were tense. His breathing was anything but relaxed. Anne wondered if he was even asleep.

She looked toward the rocks higher above, thinking about Ruben's earlier suspicion, that he had seen Keller, but Anne saw only what she had seen earlier: rock and snow.

IV

Behind the white rocks, Keller backed away. *So,* he thought, *they're both still alive.*

The initial surprise of seeing them hadn't taken long to wear off. Keller's senses and thoughts didn't seem to function the same way in this prolonged freezing cold.

He had ducked behind the rocks the moment Ruben Ramirez had turned his head toward him. Keller hoped the man hadn't seen him, but if he had, it wasn't a serious compromise. It could cost him the advantage of surprise for now, but he would find a way to regain it later.

He considered going back for Anne and Ruben, or possibly waiting for them here, but he found too many flaws in these methods of ambush. For all he knew, the two might have weapons—Javier's guns, at worst. He didn't want to risk it.

If he decided to strike, he would do it at a more opportune moment. Keller retreated to commence the next phase of his climb, moving carefully up the mountainside.

THE MOUNTAIN MYSTERY

I

ANNE DIDN'T THINK she would ever get used to the soreness. Her body wasn't used to this. Regardless, she forced herself out of the makeshift shelter. Ruben didn't stir. She put a hand on his shoulder and gave it an easy, but firm, shove.

"Ruben, wake up," she said. "We have to start climbing again." The wind had worsened. She had to lean near his ear so he could hear her.

"We have to keep moving, or we'll freeze to death."

Ruben's eyes opened. He blinked, gave her a single nod, and made a sluggish effort to climb out. Anne waited for minutes until he stood on uncertain feet in the snow.

"Are you all right to climb?" she asked. He nodded again and walked toward the upward-slanting face. She started to ask if he was sure, but stopped herself. He could decide for himself, couldn't he?

Ruben, as if hearing the passing thought in her mind, turned to her. "I'll be all right, Anne."

Anne looked up at the mountain. "I don't think we have much higher to climb," she said, although she couldn't be certain.

Ruben faced the white wall and set to anchoring himself against it for the climb. With slow motions, he resumed the upward trek. Anne resumed her advance behind him.

Numbness filled them. Instincts fueled their movements. The constant cracking of their axes surrounded them again. They pulled themselves toward a white sky, quietly grunting and gasping as they moved.

Ruben's efforts met with obvious difficulty. His vigor from earlier was far gone.

Anne's own mysterious recovery of strength still surprised her. She could only attribute it to her fierce desire to quench this burning conundrum, once Damon's and now her own.

Summoning the patchwork map from her memory was a trick that might be useful or completely useless. She didn't know yet. She didn't even know what she was looking for. She hoped she would know it when she saw it.

"Your husband must have been quite certain of something," Keller had said. *"Otherwise, you're just insane."*

Maybe Keller was right in that, she reflected. There was a narrow line between faith and desperation.

Her fingers were cold and numb. She couldn't feel her feet. The rest of her body ached. Still, she kept climbing.

II

Keller's boots crunched against the ice. His muscles heaved with his labored breaths as he dragged himself upward.

When he slipped, his heart leaped. He grabbed for the icy rocks at the lip of the ledge and held on with a squeezing mania that drove shards of ice and rock into his gloves.

He panted to catch his breath. With gradual movements, he hauled himself up and resumed the pace of his climb.

On the occasions that he reached a solid section of ground, Keller paused to study the patchwork map. He couldn't make sense of it. Either the physical exertions and extreme cold were affecting his senses or he was on the wrong mountain altogether, but that couldn't be the case. All of his other resources had been true.

If anyone would seize credit for the discoveries ahead, it would be Keller. He had done everything necessary to ensure it. His only limits were his own endurance and the meager amount of food left in his supply.

Squinting against the pale light of the sky, he realized he neared the summit. Given that, the object of his search couldn't be far away.

Once he reached another stretch of ground where he could safely plant his feet with less worry of falling, he analyzed the map again. His eyes kept returning to the three *X*'s with the question mark in parenthesis in the middle.

Keller took methodical steps up the incline. He studied his surroundings while he moved. He stopped on the snowy slope before its upturn steepened.

He stood in the same spot for minutes, looking around, trying to ascertain what had snagged his attention on some subconscious level. The wind hummed around him. After its murmur quieted, he still stood there, now gazing into the snow.

He looked again at the patchwork map. He looked around.

Keller considered his position near the white rocky protrusion that jutted from the ground at an almost-forty-five degree angle. He located the other two protruding rock formations he had seen before, white-coated rock ledges of differing heights.

Was this something of what the map's three *X's* indicated? He could find nothing else of note around here. He wouldn't have even noticed these if he hadn't been thinking about the map and trying to figure out exactly what he should be looking for.

He made steps to the approximate central area between the two ledges and the other rock structure. The ground of this area was fairly flat compared to the rest of the sloped mountain's surface. With his eyes, Keller gauged the distance to the center, though he knew this method of calculation couldn't be precise.

He paced, visually scanning the area. He saw only more snow. He stopped and stood still, his eyes continuing the search.

What now? He rubbed a gloved hand against the side of his head. Frustration penetrated the coldness that encased him.

He began to feel like a fool. A part of him wanted to erupt in an angry shout, but another part of him insisted, *No, this isn't over yet.*

Maybe it wasn't, but what could he do? He looked down at his boots and the bright snow all around them. The longer he stood here, the more resentful he became. Of what? Himself? His own failure?

He didn't know, but his anger was building and there was no one to push aside or knock down in retaliation. He saw only this gigantic mountain and a world of ice and snow, and no one to reprimand but himself. This might have been what made him angriest of all.

He dropped to a crouching position and shoveled at the snow with his hands. His knees began to hurt with an aching throb, and before long he couldn't maintain the position. He fell onto his side but continued to heave snow aside. He would be damned if he accepted the notion that he had come all this way for no reason.

When his fingers failed, Keller withdrew his ice axe and slammed it into the surface below. The axe swished through snow to connect with a harder surface. Keller grimaced at the harsh vibration through the axe's handle. Solid rock, he guessed. He gathered himself up and moved to another area to shovel more snow in the same fashion.

Again he reached rock. He spat into the snow, climbed up, and moved to another area.

A bitter taste filled Keller's mouth. He swung the axe again. In his mind, with all of his gathering rage, he swung the axe into a face. Keller couldn't place a name to the face. Maybe it didn't have a name.

He kept swinging. His arm ached. He swung harder. To his surprise, the axe head lodged into the surface with an unusual crack.

Keller stopped, confused. He tried to pull the axe back, but it stuck. He gripped the handle with both hands and jerked backward as hard as he could. The force broke the axe free and he almost flung it backward through the air.

When he recovered his balance, he discerned a

blue surface beneath the white. A crack ran through the blue barrier of ice. In the middle, where the axe's head had penetrated, he observed a narrow black opening.

Keller lowered the axe. He reached out with his other hand and felt the inner edges of the hole in the ice.

He had broken through. What had he discovered?

He gave the ice axe a look that said, *Good job. Don't fail me now!* He raised the axe and swung it again. It lodged in the ice, creating a second hole. This time, he had no difficulty in pulling it free.

A few more strikes started multiple cracks through the blue sheet of ice and into areas partially obscured beneath the snow. Keller saw the ice cracking and started backward for safer ground. Sooner than he could shift his position, the ice broke.

Keller grabbed for a handhold, but too late, and he sailed downward into darkness.

III

"Ruben," Anne called. The wind rushed across them with considerable ferocity now, and he didn't seem to hear at first.

"Ruben!"

He raised his head and wiped his nose. He was exhausted, Anne could tell, and he didn't feel well.

Anne came across the plateau where they now rested. She removed one of her gloves and touched Ruben's face with the back of her hand, and his skin was hot to the touch.

"It's all right, Ruben," Anne said to him. She leaned

close to be heard above the winds. "You can rest a minute longer if you want."

"I'll be ready soon," he breathed. He lay back against the icy stone of the wall that supported him.

"That's fine," Anne said. "We'll give it a few minutes." This wasn't the best place to rest, but she would do what she could for him. He had come this far for her, even wanting to turn back as he did. Ruben's support meant more to her than she had admitted to herself on many previous occasions throughout this awful journey.

She had put him through enough already. Ruben, who had been such a faithful friend to Damon and who had always been so good to Anne, didn't deserve this. She sat down close to him. Her thoughts roamed upward.

She didn't think their journey would take them much farther. She hadn't stopped to look at Raul's map lately, but she had struggled to hold together that mental photograph of the patchwork map. The mountain peak was closer than it had ever been. If any signs of the ancient mountain secret still existed, they were right within her grasp.

She was tired, though, and near-freezing. It had helped to keep moving. The partial shelter of the wall behind them also helped.

Ruben spoke, drawing a glance from Anne. "I just have to rest. I hope that's all right." He raised a hand to his forehead.

"That's fine, Ruben," Anne said. She sat there beside him for a few more minutes, but felt herself becoming colder and more miserable. If she didn't stand and move around, she thought, she might not be able to move her arms or legs. As it was, she couldn't seem to feel her hands and feet.

She stood up, rubbed her hands together, and paced the ledge. She studied the wall they would have to climb to continue their ascent. This wall's height extended to just above her head.

She found a bumpy, elevated section of snow-covered flat rock that allowed her to step up high enough to peek over it. The higher ground appeared to be an easy slope. She wondered how much farther it might be to the top of the mountain.

She came down from her stepstool of snowy rocks. "Ruben," she said, and touched his arm. "I think I'm going to scout ahead. I don't think we have much more until we get to the top."

She paused in thought. The details of the patchwork map were eluding her now. She imagined the cold must be chilling her brain. It might help if she could better absorb the lay of the land above.

"I won't be long," she added, because Ruben still looked at her.

"Don't worry about me," he replied. Feeling as wretched as he did, he still managed to give her a faint smile.

Anne nodded. Her concern made her departure a reluctant one. She would be quick about it, she decided.

She went into the supply pack to retrieve the camera and tucked it into a deep pocket. She took an ice axe and stepped back up to the higher section. From this point, she didn't expect a difficult climb.

She surprised herself. In less than a minute, she pulled herself up and over the edge. She made rapid steps up the next slope.

Somehow, the fatigue didn't bother her at the moment. She had almost gotten used to the aching muscles and the thin air. She didn't know that she would ever get used to the cold.

She thought she could see it in the distance, against the pale sky, the end. This quickened her steps across the land of white, blue, and occasional curious brown spot of exposed mountain rock.

If that was the highest point ahead, that meant, unless she and Ruben had strayed off-course, and unless Damon Sharpe had been wrong—a possibility she couldn't swallow—that she was close. If the patchwork map had been correct, some signs of the Mourner's Cradle must be near. She hoped she could interpret them. She couldn't know what the three *X*'s on the map represented.

When she first saw the tiny white ledge, she thought little of it. In her attempts to chisel the icy sluggishness from her memory, she stopped to look twice toward the second protruding ledge. The end of it jutted forward into a point honed by time and the elements.

She looked back to the first, similar in appearance but smaller. Not many obstacles complicated her route here. The land slanted, but she maintained her balance without difficulty.

She stopped, sensing a sudden change. She looked toward the two rock protrusions. Soon, she searched for a third, and she found it.

How she had missed it before, she didn't know. It was the largest of them all, wider and longer than the others. It extended from a lower section of the mountainside behind her rather than from a higher point.

She thought of the patchwork map and its markings. Could this be the place? Were these rocks the markers that had stood in place for ages to indicate a lost secret of the ancient world?

She looked toward the central location between the three natural structures. She could see a dark spot, but couldn't tell much else from where she stood. She moved toward it. The closer she drew, the faster she walked. She almost slid in the snow in her hurry to get there.

She exercised caution in approaching the hole in the mountainside, but couldn't hold herself back. Once close enough, she stopped to study the broken edges of the portal. Through it, she saw only blackness.

She couldn't suppress her excitement. The horrible mountain journey almost fled her mind entirely in the face of her discovery. Damon had been right. He was *right!*

She had doubted him, she acknowledged that, but she had fought against everything to defy that doubt and now she had found it at last. The mystery of this mountain was frozen in time somewhere below her very feet!

She had to go back for Ruben. He would be so thrilled to know—

Anne paused. She heard something, a strange crackling sound right beneath her.

Oh, no. She backed away from the edge of the hole, but not quickly enough. Ice and rock broke away. The hole opened wider yet, and the abyss swallowed her.

INTO DARKNESS

I

ANNE FLUNG HER arms out to grab anything she could, but found nothing in the open darkness. She screamed. There was nothing else she could do. When she hit the ground, she would die a quick death at best, or else she would break both of her legs and suffer until she perished.

She threw her arms out again and, to her surprise, caught something with one hand, but her descent was too rapid to be halted by this mere action. Her hands ripped free from the rough, rocky surface with a sharp sting.

She grabbed out again in that general direction with both hands, and her hands slapped against a solid surface. A wall? An unexpected moment later, her fingers caught onto some indented portion of the surface, almost by accident, but she latched on and fought to better secure the handhold she had gained.

Her body swung and her hands slipped away. A new wave of panic hurled through her mind. When her feet hit the ground, her mind was quick, firing a command to her body to roll and minimize the impact. Her feet crumpled, her body struck the floor, and she rolled. The force jarred her bones and teeth and filled her vision with white spots.

She had a memory-flash of her fall over the mountain ledge with Vince. It took another moment to register the hard ground against her aching body. She heaved for breath, conscious and alive and wondering just how much more of this could she take.

It smelled awful here. Something in the air, dust perhaps, choked her and she coughed. Her eyes burned and watered. She felt nauseated.

She couldn't see a thing in this darkness. Anne shook her head against the coarse ground and tried not to think too much about the fact that she was now trapped at the bottom of some dark shaft; working herself into a panic was the last thing in the world she needed to do right now.

Anne gave slow movement to her arms and legs. They hurt, but they moved. She sat up and rubbed her head. She reached out, scored her knuckles against something hard and jagged, and withdrew her hand in a hurry. She whispered a string of obscenities at no one in particular. Of the churning glob of emotions within her, anger was the easiest to cope with.

As she rubbed her hand, she heard a quiet laugh in the darkness. Anne stopped still. She was not alone here, and she recognized the quiet, self-assured laughter spilling from that mouth.

This was it. She was trapped here with *him,* and she knew there wouldn't be room for both of them.

She reached through the darkness, more careful this time, to feel a hard wall with a spiny surface. She moved her hands to the left of it and found empty space. She rose to her feet, taking care to make as little noise as possible.

If Anne couldn't see, Keller probably couldn't. She would wait for him to make a sound and divulge his location. She didn't know whether he was armed. She knew she wasn't. The only advantage she could gain here was that of surprise.

A blinding light pierced her vision. It came from a flashlight, and the flashlight was in Keller's hand as he came toward her.

She rushed aside and stumbled on the previously-unseen bones littering the floor. Her balance escaped her. The bones clattered to the side, and she went to the floor. She threw her hands out at the last second. Her palms struck the ground and bruised against the solid rock.

"Why, hello, Mrs. Sharpe," Keller said, the pale light of the beam outlining his grin. Anne grabbed the first and only thing she saw, a bone. She hurled it at him.

Keller threw up an arm and ducked. The bone struck his forearm and bounced.

Anne saw fury in his lips and eyes. He stepped forward and delivered a brutal kick. She raised her legs to deflect it, but her angle was wrong. His boot cracked into her back. She cried out.

Before she could react further, Keller grabbed her legs in one arm and swept them aside. He moved in close and grabbed her hair. He yanked it hard. A hiss of pain left her dry lips. Keller's other hand latched onto her throat. She struggled against his choking fingers as they dug into her windpipe until she gagged.

She struggled in vain. He didn't relent. He

squeezed harder, snarling down at her with a face like a beast's, his cracked lips curled in a sneer with teeth showing.

She fought the paralyzing panic and swung at his hand, but she didn't have much leverage or strength. She struck the side of his head. The feeble effort accomplished little.

Her other hand found an object nearby, another bone. She swung it. It wasn't heavy enough to cause any true damage and did nothing to deter him.

Keller's eyes narrowed. Anne's mind filled with fog. The bone in her hand wasn't wieldy as a bludgeon, but through her fog she perceived its end which came to a sharp point. She could barely think but acted on instinct, pulling the sharp-tipped bone back to stab at him.

She drove the point into his arm. He screamed and released her. She gasped for breath. Her senses were confused, but she knew she couldn't delay. The sharp bone had fallen from her grasp. She grabbed for it again and thrust it toward him. The motion accomplished nothing. He had already backed away, and looked down to inspect his red, wet forearm.

Anne scrambled to her feet and launched herself toward him. Keller was quicker than she anticipated. He sidestepped and caught her around the midsection. She stabbed out with the bone-knife, missing. Keller flung her at a wall. She tried to stop, but her legs weren't strong enough to obey the command. Her arms struck the wall first. The wall's spiky spines stuck into her skin. She gasped. Blood ran from the fresh cuts in her arms. The bone fled her grasp, rattling to the ground.

She pulled herself from the wall and found herself

looking right into Keller's face. He seized her by both arms and slammed her backward. The sharp spines jabbed into her back and she screamed. Keller pressed her hard against the wall, and the spines bored into her flesh. She could only gasp.

"Bitch," he said. He spat in her face. The thick saliva slid down the side of her nose and drilled down her lips.

He had her pinned, but she kept struggling. She could still muster enough free movement to shove her face right into his, and she bit down, her teeth crunching into the bridge of his nose. Keller screamed in her face. He punched her head. Dazed, she held on, biting deeper. His coppery blood flowed over her tongue.

She freed her arms, but before she could think to do anything else, he punched her again in the side of her head. She collapsed.

Incredulous, Keller grabbed his nose. Blood gushed from it.

On the ground at his feet, Anne saw the pointed bone. She went for it. Once her fingers closed around the bone-knife, she raised it to slam the sharp end sideways into Keller's ankle. He shouted and tried to leap back, but the awkward movement failed him and the point pierced flesh and muscle. His steps awry, Keller fell to the ground.

Anne gripped the bone in a tight fist. The light still illuminated their portion of the area, but she didn't see Keller anymore.

A few seconds later, her eyes located him. He scrambled into the dark, toward a distant corner, away from the flashlight's greater beam.

Anne climbed to her feet and looked across the bones that covered the floor. She spotted a longer one with a jagged, sharp end. She snatched it up, dropped the other, and stared across the length of the cavern toward the man who crawled away.

"Oh, Mr. Keller?" Anne called, her tone buoyant. "Leaving so soon, my dear? I don't think so."

A chilling smile crossed her thin lips. With the bone-blade in her hands, she went after him.

II

Keller heard her footsteps coming. He tried to move faster, but pain fired through his senses.

She approached from behind. She stood over him and thought of all of the pain he had caused. This wasn't about her, though. This was about Damon, the man she loved. Would he still be here if not for this bastard? It was just possible.

A seething hatred akin to what she had felt on the day of her husband's funeral welled up in her.

Keller had stopped crawling. With a dark corner of the cavern ahead, he had nowhere else to go. She had him. Anne looked down at the bone in her hand and ran one finger across its sharp end.

She crouched beside Keller's prone form. She reached into his hair with her free hand, grabbed a handful, and gripped it tightly. She yanked his head back. He winced.

She pressed the bone's sharp edge against the soft flesh of his exposed throat. Keller's eyes, looking upward, saw her.

Keller stared into the face that had haunted his

dreams for years. It had many forms, the face of his failure, though he hadn't been able to give it a name until now.

Anne Sharpe saw the fear in Keller's eyes right before she slit his throat.

THE PIT OF BONES

KELLER'S LIFE DRAINED across the cavern floor. His final wet choking sounds faded away. Anne had cut deep. It didn't take long.

She waited for the peace to wash through her now that this man, the one who had made it his life's mission to ruin her husband's life, who had tried to kill Ruben and her, died at last. The peace didn't come, but silence did.

She stood and looked over the blood-tipped bone in her hand. She tossed it aside. Looking up, she saw a point of light.

The tunnel that she, and presumably Keller, had fallen through appeared to be a twisting one. It seemed unusual that she could have fallen straight downward without striking solid rock at some point, but here she was at the bottom of the deep pit, injured, but still standing.

Shining the flashlight around, she spotted a supply pack against one wall and knew it had to be Keller's. She walked over to it.

At least he had brought his supplies. She had nothing.

Would Ruben come for her? Surely he would. She

THE MOURNER'S CRADLE

hoped he could find her. This had begun as a simple scouting effort, but now this place had trapped her.

She stared upward through the twisting vertical tunnel and shouted. If Ruben was anywhere up there, she hoped he would hear.

"Ruben!" she shouted to the distant light above. Her voice echoed through the darkness and no answer came.

She looked back to the floor, and at the supply pack. She crouched down to dig through it. There were a couple of bags of food, she discovered, and some climbing tools. The ice axe might not be of any use here since most of this place was solid rock, but one never knew when the extra tools might become useful in some other way.

She discovered a bunched wad of line in the pack. Maybe she could find a way to climb out of this hole.

She found a crumpled piece of paper inside, beneath everything else. *The patchwork map.* She held it in front of her and observed it by the light of the flash beam.

She examined the drawings of the mountain terrain, the layout of the mountain face they had climbed, its various ledges and areas of stable ground, and the three *X*'s that surrounded that question mark, what Damon thought to be the location of the Mourner's Cradle—where she stood right now.

Bones strewed the ground everywhere around her, more bones than she had first noticed. She saw skulls, the bones of arms, legs, and ribs, and other bones she couldn't fully identify. They were human bones, she did know this, and this pit had to be a mass grave or a death trap. For her, it might be both, unless she could find an escape. Her eyes traveled across the remains of the dead.

Was this what she had come to find? There must be more, she thought. She walked across the cavernous chamber, studying everything within it.

Little remained of this region's oldest cultures for the modern world to decipher. There was the crude architecture, and of course the knotted cords of the quipu, but little else aside from the strong-standing natural landmarks that had weathered the passing of time, such as the three prominent rock formations that surrounded this tomb in the mountain.

As such, there was no writing of any sort on these walls and no indication that it had ever been anything but a place to abandon the dead. One of Damon's favorite theories, Anne recalled, was that the Mourner's Cradle had been a graveyard.

Why had he been so captivated by it? Shouldn't the Mourner's Cradle be something more than *just* a graveyard? Shouldn't there be something besides this pit of bones and the silence that filled it?

She didn't know. She remembered the camera and reached into her pockets for it, but was stunned to find it in pieces, destroyed by the fall.

Anne paced. She studied the walls, the areas where the ceiling dipped lower and where the higher reaches extended up toward the light of the surface. Below, from among the pit's many, many bones, a vacant skull grinned up at her.

It wasn't smiling, she corrected her imagination. It was dead, like everything here. There was nothing, absolutely nothing, but death here.

Why had she come? Why?

She looked at the fragmented camera in her hand. Its pieces tumbled from her hand.

She continued pacing the room and kicked bones aside. The silence stretched, broken only by the clattering of bones.

She couldn't ignore the growing pressure in her chest. The glances she cast around were quick and unfocused. Her mind roamed elsewhere again.

She thought about Damon. She thought about the journey, about everything he had thrown away for this, what the two of them had lost together in their final years because of it.

Was all of this worth it? Was this nothingness worth everything she had lost?

"No," she whispered. She looked at the flashlight's beam. It flickered.

There was nothing in this cave of bones and there was nothing for her to go back to but an empty house in St. Charles. Besides that, what was left?

The skull kept staring. The flashlight's beam went out.

Anne dropped to the cold floor in the darkness and screamed.

INTO WHITE

I

RUBEN OPENED HIS eyes. He thought he might have heard something. A heavy sleep weighed on him. He struggled feebly to hold it at bay.

Who was there? Was it Anne?

He drew a slow breath. He waited for Anne to come into view. She never did.

Maybe he had only been hearing things, deceiving murmurs of the wind. He had a strange feeling then, a feeling that Anne hadn't returned coupled with the feeling that he might never see her again.

He hoped she was all right. He had no way of knowing.

Ruben's thoughts meandered, and he stared into white.

II

The passing of time was impossible for Anne to gauge in the darkness of the hole. She waited there at its bottom, alone with her thoughts in the surrounding blackness. She could hardly bear it. She had to get out of this place. Anne searched for some sense of direction through the dark pit, and almost lost her footing several times on the bones covering the ground.

The flashlight flickered on and off. She shook it until the faint beam came on again. She took Keller's supply pack and did the only thing she could think of doing. She began her efforts to climb toward the faraway light above.

She found rough areas in the rocky walls, protrusions, orifices, anything she could use for a handhold or foothold, and pulled herself upward inch-by-inch. More than once it felt as if her hands might slip, but each time, she seized another hold and continued to move upward.

She ascended for a considerable distance before the climb became truly difficult, the upward tunnel becoming winding and precarious. She sustained more cuts on her hands and arms from the sharper rocks, but the pain remained dull and distant.

The thought of bleeding to death in this place didn't bother her. If she died here, it was for the best. Somewhere inside, she almost wished it. Meanwhile, she continued climbing, although the light didn't appear to be coming any closer.

When the climbing became even more treacherous, she imagined she might fall to her death soon, but somehow she clung on with bleeding hands and continued up through the turning tunnel.

As she climbed, it became colder, reminding her of the icy temperatures she had become accustomed to during much of the mountain journey with Ruben. The freezing winds of that cold place would return again soon.

Ruben hadn't come. He was probably out searching for her. She hoped there was some way he could make everything right, something he could say to her. Oh, how she hoped as she climbed toward the light.

III

Escaping the hole proved a tricky affair, but she kept moving, her body almost acting of its own accord like a mechanical puppet. Somehow, she persisted. When she emerged to the surface, the ice surrounding the hole cracked further. She scurried away before it opened wide and threatened to take her down again.

A gust of cold high-mountain air brought on a dizzying sickness. She grasped her head. It throbbed now. The dizziness almost overwhelmed her.

She dropped to her knees and crawled forward. Her stomach twisted. She heaved, but nothing came up. After a minute of this, her stomach relaxed, but it still felt awful. She wiped her mouth, although she hadn't vomited. She looked up to the white sky and tried to stand.

She came to her feet again and felt the cold spreading through her legs. She paused to reorient herself before wearily half-stumbling down the snowy slope.

She almost went right over the edge but saw it within the last moment. When she looked down, she could see the next ledge down and the rocks she had ascended to reach this higher ground.

She climbed down with awkward, slippery progress. She slid down to the rocks and almost fell in her efforts to return to the flatter ground of the plateau below.

Ruben sat there in the snow, in the same spot as before. She approached him. "Ruben?" she spoke.

She saw no trace of movement from him. She watched his chest for motion, and saw none.

"Ruben," she said, shaking him.

She took one of his icy hands and reached out with some hesitation to touch his face. She pulled in a deep breath and sat down beside him. Her mind whirled through the journey they had shared and through everything before that.

"Ruben," she whispered. "I'm so sorry."

She brought his cold hand to her face and pressed against it. She closed her eyes and leaned into him. Quiet tears rolled down her face. Silence swallowed the time.

When the winds increased, she opened her eyes. She stood, and from the overlook, she gazed across the white lands and slopes below, expanses she saw no end to.

Anne took one of the green supply packs, as she didn't seem to have Keller's anymore, and started down the mountain.

IV

Intermittently, the freezing air, snow, and cold stone penetrated Anne's consciousness. More than once, she faltered in her numb downward climb.

She remembered the camera, destroyed with everything else. With it, Damon had taken photos of her. Its first photograph had been of her, as it happened. It had been almost accidental, though Anne suspected he had done it on purpose.

She had watched him fumble with the camera until he snapped the picture that would feature her with arms crossed and lips downturned in a slight frown. The camera's flash had startled her.

"Damon," she chastised him afterward, and shook her head.

The memory dissipated into the vastness below. Another memory, another photograph, filled the void.

Ruben had taken this one. Damon and Anne stood in front of their house. They had only just bought it and hadn't even moved in yet, but it became their home for many years. On the lawn in front of the white-painted house, Damon held Anne close, his face pressing into her hair.

This summoned the memory of another photograph, this one from their trip to Lima the year before. Ruben had not accompanied them then, and the picture was taken by the gracious father of a small family outside the Museo Larco.

Anne stood with Damon outside the building's exterior. He stood near to her, lightly touching the small of her back. He looked straight at the camera, a pleasant smile on his lips. Anne gazed downward, but a slight smile adorned her face.

A strong, freezing wind struck her. Her bruised hands burned against the ice and rock, but she continued climbing down. Her mind again retreated into the memories of a different life.

She and Damon sat close together on their tan sofa, the soft light of their brass lamp nearby, a whiskey-and-cola in Damon's hand and Anne with her hands in her lap and her face turned toward Damon. Ruben stood a short distance away, at the edge of the photo with one hand in his pocket and the other holding his own iced-down mixed drink.

In another photograph, Damon sat buried among his stacks of books. Next to a messy stack of brown and blue folders and loose papers, a glass of water with melting ice formed a moisture ring on the cluttered desk. A thin chain dangled from the room's small single-bulb fixture above, which cast a dim light across Damon's work space. In the background, large maps adorned the white walls.

Anne couldn't remember that specific night, but she remembered the photograph, clearly one taken during those last strained months of their life together. A photograph was a glimpse of a life, an instant frozen in time, and the truth was more complicated than an instant could allow or a moment's expression could reveal.

Anne and Damon's relationship had been far from perfect, but for a time, at least they had seemed perfect for one another.

Another series of photographs flooded through Anne's thoughts, the final photographs, the artifacts and ruins of a buried world.

The camera's fragments lay scattered across a stillness of death. Damon was gone, and so was Ruben, and almost everything else, it seemed, but the memories, and the snow, ice, and rock amid the coldness.

GHOST OF THE PAST

I

SHE CAME ALONE from the mountains. Thin, frail, and ashen, she appeared the ghost of a woman.

The people of the small countryside village watched her as they had before. They didn't recognize her from the previous occasion. She spoke little, only dropping a few items in trade for provisions.

They muttered among themselves. Those who passed her closely enough saw something in her eyes they could not comprehend, and it disturbed them. Was it madness? Evil? Who or what was this woman and where had she come from?

They were happy to see her go. Her presence frightened the children.

In other towns along her route, she stirred similar reactions. Some were openly guarded. Others kept their eyes averted and lips sealed. Many maintained their distance.

In contrast, few noticed her on the crowded streets of Lima. It was the same within the airport unless she presented herself in a direct fashion, as she had to do when securing a flight back to her home country of the United States of America.

Anne looked at the ticket in her hand. This was it, then? Back to St. Charles? So read her ticket. She hadn't even considered it until after the destination quietly fell from her lips. She supposed there was nowhere else to go.

The longer she waited, the more she thought of St. Charles as the last place on earth she wanted to see again, but she had already made her choice. There wasn't much money left and she didn't care to make the effort of trying to change her flight. There was about as much for her anywhere else as there was back in St. Charles.

The difference was that in St. Charles, the rubble of her life awaited her. Damon's grave was there, along with a house full of emptiness.

Anne noticed the absence of her wedding ring again, then she saw the traces of Keller's blood beneath her nails. She retreated to the bathroom to wash her hands. No matter how many times she scrubbed the soap into them and rinsed, she couldn't wash it completely away.

She had killed a man. She cut his throat with gusto.

She remembered the brutal compulsions she felt in that pit of bones. The malice ran deep in her. She had never realized how deep until then.

She had reveled in Keller's blood. She had looked into his eyes and cut his throat wide open. Now she had only this hollow numbness.

A dark-featured woman washed her hands at the next sink. She watched Anne. Anne became conscious of it and glanced over. When their eyes met, the woman jerked away and turned to leave.

Anne walked out of the restroom and returned to

her seat. She looked to the clock more than once. It seemed frozen still.

She wondered how much of a person's life was spent waiting on others. A lot, she imagined, but did it make any amount of difference either way? What was the rush? What was the use?

If only she had died while climbing that mountain, Ruben could have turned back. He might still be alive. Anne wouldn't have discovered that dark hole, and she wouldn't be sitting here knowing that Damon had spent his final years chasing an empty hole until he was finally buried in one.

The pit of bones could yield some archaeological value, but Anne had little certainty of such things. Damon would have, if he still lived. With the camera crushed to bits, Anne had no photographs, only the chilling memory. She could call Cornwell, but why should she? He didn't deserve to know. Besides, she didn't know if he would even believe her. If he ever decided he cared again, let him find out for himself.

In the end, Anne would probably take the knowledge to her grave.

She looked at the clock again, and around at the various other people who waited. Some read to pass the time. Some looked around as she did. One family sat in near-silence. In another section, a mother with frizzy brown hair scolded her screaming child.

The bags beneath the mother's eyes declared a lack of sleep. Though exasperated, the woman continued the quiet scolding, but the child ignored her and kept screaming and crying.

Anne clenched her teeth and stared at the noisemakers until the personnel called her flight.

II

Anne arrived in St. Charles in mid-afternoon. She shuffled out of the plane among a disarrayed line of other passengers.

She stepped back onto the open floor of the St. Charles Regional Airport. For seconds on end, she stood there, until at last she started along its length toward a glass panel at the edge of the perimeter to look outside. It was a cloudy day, but there was no rain.

She retrieved what remained of her luggage, only the tattered green supply pack. It contained everything she had left. She had a fleeting thought of the old black-and-blue duffel bag with its torn bottom, well since discarded. Everything she had managed to salvage from it she had jammed into the bottom of the supply pack with all of the other junk.

She lugged the supply pack toward a bench, where she took a seat. With the pack resting next to her legs, she watched the people walk by.

These people in the airport had busy lives, somewhere to go. Anne had an empty house.

She stood, lifted the supply pack, and walked to the airport café to order a coffee. She couldn't remember the last time she ate anything, so she ordered a muffin.

Her thoughts wound between an equally dismal past and future. She forced her attention to the black surface of the coffee. It reminded her of the coffee Ruben had made for them in the ice cave on the mountain.

She brought herself to take a drink, but the coffee

was cold by the time she did and she couldn't even taste it.

She nibbled at the edge of the muffin. The soft crumbs mixed with her saliva to become a dull paste in her mouth. She worked it out of her mouth with her tongue and oozed it onto a napkin, which she squeezed into a wad and set on the table.

The next time she raised her head, she caught the young man behind the counter looking toward her. He turned away in an impromptu effort to pretend he hadn't been staring.

"Your muffin tastes like shit, by the way," Anne called across the room to him.

"Ma'am?" he replied, now looking back at her.

She snatched up the muffin and flung it across the room at him. Startled, he ducked. The muffin bounced off the wall behind the counter.

With a bit of caution, he stood back up. "I'll have to ask you to leave," he said.

"Or what?" Anne asked. She stood up, took her cup of coffee in one hand, and approached the counter.

The young man's eyes widened. He fumbled for words but floundered, and flinched as if afraid she would throw the coffee at him. Anne stopped near the counter to affix him with a cold gaze.

She clinked the cup of coffee down on the counter. She raised her eyes to his pale, acne-ridden face once more before she abruptly walked out of the café.

Anne crossed the airport and exited through the glass front doors, stepping back out to the suddenly-not-so-familiar streets of St. Charles. The sky was gray. The air was stale to her.

She couldn't remember where she had parked the

car. She wandered between rows of vehicles for almost ten minutes before spotting the small gray car.

She dropped the supply pack and dug through her pockets until she found the keys. After all she had been through, it came as a mild surprise when she discovered she still had them. She stuck the key in, opened the door, climbed into the car, and turned the key in its ignition.

Click. Nothing. She turned the key again. *Click.*

It wouldn't start. She stepped back out, slammed the door, and went back into the airport to call a taxi.

Some undeterminable time later, a blue cab pulled up to the curbside. Anne climbed into the back and mumbled the address to the driver, an older man with silver hair.

Anne looked out the side window as the cab rolled away. After the initial minutes melted away, the cab moved down a vacant street and turned up one of the main stretches through downtown St. Charles. After another two turns, they entered her neighborhood.

The cab slowed and turned onto her street. It coasted toward the home she and Damon had shared for twelve years.

Anne's hands squeezed into fists. Her nails bit into her skin. The cab pulled toward the side of the road, stopping beside the house's front lawn.

"Keep going," she said. The cab driver cast questioning eyes at her through the rear-view mirror.

"I said," Anne said, her patience evaporating in the span of a second, "to keep going."

The driver applied a gentle acceleration. He drove past the rest of the houses to the end of the street. Before he could ask, Anne said, "Take a right."

When they neared the end of the next street, she said, "A right."

Before much longer, the cab moved along her street again. She regarded the house again. She thought about climbing out of the cab, walking up to the house and opening the front door, but she couldn't. To walk back into that place and pretend it was home again, to live alone in that empty house and carry on as if the past month, the past years of her life had never even happened . . .

The cab had stopped, she realized. "Just keep driving," she told the cab driver again. He started the cab along the street again. The man thought she was crazy, no doubt. She didn't care what he thought. His thoughts, or anyone else's, were the least of her concerns.

She wouldn't come back here again.

The cab driver glanced uncertainly at her through the mirror, but he didn't question her directions even when they took them in complete circles. The fare was Anne's to pay.

Anne didn't know whether she even had the money to pay it. She just sat in the back of the cab, blood on her hands and oblivion in her thoughts, and rode toward an unknown destination.

DOWNTOWN

I

ON AN OUTER edge of St. Charles, just before the downtown area thinned toward the outskirts, the flickering neon sign of the King's Motel burned against the night. For Anne, cheap rooms were the motel's prime selling point. She had almost two hundred dollars in cash left.

The mustached man behind the counter, whose name tag read *Mike*, pretended not to see her at first. She stood waiting for almost a minute before he raised his head to regard her for an expressionless moment.

"Can I help you?" he asked.

"I need a room," she said.

"How many nights?"

"One. For now."

"Eight dollars."

Anne lowered the green pack onto the floor and crouched to open it. She sorted through it until she came up with seven crumpled dollar bills, which she tossed onto the counter along with a handful of change. Mike blew audibly through his nostrils. He took the money and slid a key onto the counter.

"Room 26," Mike said, and turned his attention elsewhere.

Anne took the key and exited the lobby. The lobby was separate from the motel rooms which were accessible from rows of red-painted doors outside. She found the door marked 26 and pushed the key in, popping the door open.

She stepped into the off-white-walled room, shut the door behind her, and locked it. She tossed the supply pack down and sat on the edge of the bed.

She leaned over to open the lone supply pack. To her surprise, she found the switchblade, once Vince's, bundled with the grimy clothing inside the pack. She hadn't tried to bring the knife as carry-on luggage, of course; she hadn't realized she still had it until now. How had she failed to notice it there before?

She threw the knife aside and flopped back onto the bouncy mattress and frayed comforter. She stared at the dirty yellow ceiling and the cracks lining it. Anne smelled traces of mildew and cigarette smoke.

Sleep felt impossible. Discomfort gnawed at her stomach.

The last time she had tried to eat, back in the airport café, it hadn't gone well. She didn't have an appetite, but she needed something to fill the emptiness in her stomach and the hours of silence.

Anne climbed up from the bed and again noticed the discarded switchblade on the cheap brown carpeting. She tucked it into her clothing and concealed it before walking outside and closing the motel room door behind her.

She didn't come to this part of town often, but she

THE MOURNER'S CRADLE

remembered a run-down burger shack not far from the King's Motel. She followed the street toward it.

The lack of customers in its dying inner light didn't deter her. She took a table in the back and browsed the selection. Red and brown spots of dried sauce stuck to the front of the tan paper menu. A server, a gum-smacking woman with big blond hair and a blue ribbon in her hair, appeared with a pad of paper and a pen.

Anne ordered a regular hamburger, no cheese, no onions, no tomatoes, no anything. She sipped on a glass of water until the server brought the plate to her table. The woman slid it in front of Anne, smacked her bubblegum, and walked away without a word.

Anne tried to eat it, but mostly kept sipping at her water. She felt nausea rising.

The server roamed near the table again. Anne lifted her glass of water and brought it down with a heavy thud.

"Check, please," she said. The server glanced at her but kept walking.

She returned a few minutes later with the check. Anne hurried to pay for the awful meal and pushed out the door. She vomited in the parking lot and stumbled away, dizzy. She stopped, holding her head for a minute, until she recovered enough to walk back toward the motel. She hoped she could make it that far. She didn't feel good.

Along the dark street, she heard something and looked to her right. She gazed at a wall of darkness. A sense of caution arose in her, but her dulled state of mind suppressed the tension she might otherwise have felt. She felt a sense of security in the switchblade. Anne placed a hand against it but waited, listening.

A gray tabby cat walked out. It stopped, watching her. After a few seconds, it bolted away. Anne watched it go and resumed her walk.

She had a thought of Tabby Reinhart and considered giving Tabby a call, saying "meow, meow" into the phone, and hanging up. It was stupid, but the idea amused her when nothing else did.

Once back in the King's Motel, she had forgotten whatever silly notion it was that came to her minutes before and instead threw herself into a shower. She did her best to ignore the grimy green shower tiles. The bath towels seemed crusty. *The King's Motel, indeed,* she thought. What kind of king would stay in a place like this? The King of the Cockroaches?

After the shower, she felt dirtier than before. She toweled off her hair and without a glance at herself in the bathroom mirror, she returned to the bedroom, fell into bed, and lost consciousness.

II

Sunlight streamed through a crack in the curtains. Anne opened her eyes, winced, and turned away from the piercing light. After another hour, she dragged herself out of bed.

She threw on a set of clothes. She didn't feel like going outside, but staying in the motel room by herself soon proved awful. This morning, the room felt tiny and oppressive to her, like a prison cell.

She shoved herself into action, leaving the motel room and wandering up the street toward a small grocery store she had spotted earlier. The walk took mere minutes, but the minutes seemed endless. The store's beige exterior had no windows and reminded her of an oversized storage shed.

Inside, the gray-haired, unshaven man behind the counter looked at her but didn't speak. Anne entered one of the aisles to find assorted products squashed together on the shelves. Boxes of macaroni, cans of sardines, mustard—the longer she looked, the less any of it appealed to her.

She eventually settled on a box of soda crackers. She needed something she could stomach. She took the box to the front and tossed it onto the counter along with a few more wadded dollars.

Going back to her motel room, she tried to eat some of the crackers. They were too dry, and she couldn't easily choke them down. She spat them into the small metal trash can in the corner of the room and sat on the edge of the bed until the sickness spiraled in her stomach again.

At least this time she had a toilet. She rushed into the tiny bathroom and threw up into the bowl.

She didn't bother to rinse her mouth at the sink. She hardly tasted the acidic scum that lined the inside of her mouth. She stumbled back to the bed and dropped onto it.

Had she paid for tonight's stay? She couldn't remember. Performing such a simple task seemed like a complicated ordeal not worth addressing.

Anne ran her tongue around in her mouth and collected a few dismal lumps of vomit. Turning her head, she spat them across the bed, speckling the top sheet with orange and pink.

Why had she come back to St. Charles? To die? So she could be buried with her husband? The King's

Motel wasn't that far from Marion Cemetery, as it happened, though the choice in motels hadn't been deliberate on any obvious level.

She thought back to Damon's funeral and all of the people who were there. Where were those people now? Where were they when Damon was alive? What a joke.

Ruben was there, but Anne didn't want to think about Ruben right now. And Tabby, Tabby Reinhart. Tabby had been there, she remembered, for whatever that was worth. Hadn't Anne thought about calling Tabby earlier?

Moving slowly, Anne rounded the bed to the bedside telephone, and picked it up to dial the number.

"Hello?" a woman's voice answered.

"Tabby, is that you?"

"This is Tabby Reinhart. Who is this?"

"Really, Tabby. You don't know who this is?"

Tabby hesitated. "Anne?" she said with uncertainty.

"It's me," Anne said, her voice almost a whisper.

"You—well, you don't sound like yourself." Tabby sighed. "I'm sorry, Anne. How are you?"

"Miserable."

"Is there anything I can do?"

"I think I might be dying."

"What do you mean? What's happening over there? Where are you?"

"King's Motel."

"What are you doing there?"

"I wouldn't know where to begin." Anne almost hung up the phone, but paused. "Tabby?"

"Yes?"

"Meow."

Anne hung up the phone and fell back on the bed. Her head hurt.

Someone knocked at the door. Anne drew in a hard breath and blew it out.

The knocking returned. "Go away," Anne whispered. She heard the jingling of keys in the lock.

"Housekeeping!" a high-pitched voice called from the other side of the door. Anne's body tensed with anger.

"Go away!" she screamed. "Leave me alone!"

III

Inside the small hotel room, Anne Sharpe hid away from the city and the world.

She couldn't always tell whether she was dreaming or awake. Sometimes she saw the interior of her abandoned home. On occasion, she saw Damon there, but more often the house was empty as it had been in the days after his death.

There were moments when she saw a dark hole in a distant mountainside. Though she wanted to forget, she could never keep her mind far from that place beneath the cold, white mountainside. She had learned a lot about herself in that silent pit of bones.

Other times, she found herself in an eight-dollar motel room. On the chipped brown stand beside the bed perched a digital alarm clock with a radio. Earlier, she had felt a compulsion to destroy the silence and switched the radio on. Right now, "Summer Breeze" by Seals and Crofts played.

When Anne thought about the past, she acknowledged there were many ways it might have gone differently, but the time for decisions was over. She had long since made that decision to trust and support Damon in his studies, and it angered her that he had used most days of their final years together on such drivel. She should have said something, done something, but she hadn't.

It was hard to hate him. Anne was as guilty as he was. She had carried on his foolish pursuit and took it so much farther when she dragged Ruben up into those mountains to die.

Keller had died, but it didn't bring Damon or Ruben back. It didn't accomplish anything. It was just an act of hatred and murder. Even if Keller had tried to kill her, he had been on the ground, near-helpless when Anne had sliced his throat open.

For the path she had chosen, Anne knew herself too well now. She knew what she deserved.

She stirred from the bed, needing to use the bathroom.

She slipped a leg over one side and slid over its edge until her foot touched the fuzzy floor. She pulled herself along until her other foot was over the edge. When both feet were against the floor, she leaned forward to stand and almost fell right over.

It took a moment's concentration to force her muscles into complacency. She straightened her legs and sidled forward, breathing heavily.

She saw the switchblade on the floor. She gripped the side of the bed to lower herself to the carpet, where she picked up the knife. Beneath the cheap motel room lighting, she examined it. The blade was sticky with residue. Blood?

She pushed into the bathroom and sat down to do

her business. She flushed, rose, and leaned over the sink.

She still heard the music coming from the other room, but her attention didn't stray from the switchblade. She held it in both palms and took the handle-end of it with her fingers.

She placed the blade's cool metal edge against her wrist. She raised her face to look into the mirror.

Her face was pale, her hair thin, and her eyes tired. The longer she looked at her malnourished, ugly countenance, the more she felt drawn to her own eyes. She blinked. A slow trickle of incredulity leaked through her thoughts.

She tucked the blade away and leaned toward the mirror for a closer look. She braced herself against the bathroom counter with both hands and leaned even closer, staring at her reflection.

She saw something strange in her eyes and studied it, searching her mind for an answer. What had happened to her?

When had she truly felt different? When had she become this husk of misery?

Her thoughts plunged back into that pit of bones. She remembered the fear she felt there, but even more so, the uncontrollable hatred that had magnified within. Her emotions had flooded her into a turbulent, devastating transformation.

Something awful existed in that pit. She knew that now. Even if she didn't comprehend the force that endured in that place of darkness, it had affected her. Because of it, she had lost almost everything.

At an earlier time in her life, she might have laughed at such nonsense, but not now, as she looked into the mirror and saw the yellow madness that flecked the natural brown of her irises.

With the sudden shaking, she removed her hands from the edges of the sink with a start, but soon realized *she* wasn't shaking. It was the mirror, the sink, everything around her.

HOUR OF DESTRUCTION

I

ANNE STUMBLED OUT of her motel room. The sickness lurched in her again with another sudden bout of dizziness. Coupled with the unsteady ground, it almost staggered her.

The vibrations in the ground were no delusions. They were as real as the cold feeling that gripped her inside.

Why the ground shook, she couldn't begin to guess. Of the rest, Anne suspected, she was dying.

That exhausting climb into the mountains, the loss suffered, and her experience in the pit had not been altogether in vain. The secret of that place was inside her, changing her. She had merely failed to realize it until now.

Many of the motel's other customers stood outside. The vibrations beneath their feet and the rattling of mirrors, windows, and anything that wasn't bolted down had driven them out. Undistracted by the shouts and excited conversations all around, Anne stumbled away from the King's Motel.

Her feet reached the hard street. She followed the long, dark stretch but couldn't be certain whether she moved in the right direction until she saw the road to her right, one lined with elm trees. Near the gates at its end, the road's pavement met a narrower path of dark soil and led into Marion Cemetery.

Even this late, the gates stood open as they had on the day Lucy Newcomb heard the whispers and laid the flowers upon her aunt's grave.

When Anne reached the cemetery's entrance, she almost collapsed. She caught herself on the black iron bar of one of the gates and pulled herself up.

She clung to the gate until she felt able to walk again, and despite the feeling that the ground might buckle beneath her, she moved through the gates into the cemetery.

On a grave marked *Newcomb,* the sunflowers and daisies had long since wilted and blown away in the wind. Anne managed her way past this grave and several others before she fell to the dirt.

She knew the unmarked grave in front of her, her husband's grave, though she had never been here. She crawled forward and laid her head against the cool, smooth pad of dirt.

The city quivered around her. She couldn't make sense of it but didn't care enough to try. The world could burn.

She closed her eyes. Sleep took her on her husband's grave.

||

On any typical day, the length of river coursing through the valley region made a prime spot for fishing. Today was not a typical day.

For much of the day, no one caught any fish from the silent river. During the night, the water's surface rippled in the moonlight.

One fisherman, a stubborn man who had decided he wouldn't go home without a catch, stood by the riverside. In the soft, silver moonlight, he saw the irregular pattern glinting from the water's surface and frowned.

"That's not—" the fisherman began, but stopped short. He lifted his brown cap to scratch the dry scalp underneath.

He stepped closer. His boots squished in the mud. He paused to steady his balance, extended both arms, and lowered himself to a crouch to better examine the water's surface.

"Something's not right," he said. No fish today at all, and now this?

Someone shouted from afar, diverting his attention. When he stood to full height and turned, a rock shifted beneath one of his boots. His foot slid in the mud and he sprawled into the mud and water with a heavy splash. His arm raked against a rock. He raised his arm to inspect the bloody, muddy scrape across his skin.

The water's rippling intensified. About that time, the fisherman felt the ground trembling.

He slid around for another moment before scampering to his feet and hauling himself, covered in mud, away from the bank. He remembered the shouting and craned his head toward its source.

Another of the valley's residents held an anxious exchange with one of his neighbors. Farther along, he saw others grouped together in frantic conversation. Had they all noticed the same disturbances he had?

He felt the vibrations through his boots and hurried away from the bank. He didn't know what was happening, but he felt safer surrounded by solid ground.

With his eyes to the ground, he straightened his hat. Without knowing why, the fisherman looked back at the river and along its length toward the white-lit outline of the River Bridge spanning it in the distance.

III

Francine Everett looked into the rear-view mirror and rubbed blush onto her cheeks. She reached for the mascara and shot a quick glance back at the road in time to see the white Chrysler Cordoba ahead of her brake hard. She tensed and punched her own brakes. Her tires squealed. The makeup kit fell into her lap and tumbled to the floorboard. Her blue '79 Porsche screeched to a stop just shy of the other vehicle's back bumper.

"What the hell?" Francine spurted, glaring through the front windshield.

The traffic light turned green. The white Cordoba drove on. Annoyed, Francine reached down to the floorboard to locate the makeup kit. Once she found it, she slid it into the passenger's seat and accelerated, soon gaining on the other car again.

"Oh, come on already!" she exclaimed.

Didn't they realize some people had places to be? She hoped they would keep going straight since the next turn was hers, but the vehicle turned right.

"No such luck," Francine muttered. She turned onto the River Bridge after the other vehicle and pushed close to it.

The tires of her Porsche bumped across the River Bridge. Between the rough asphalt beneath the tires and her close attention to the slow-moving vehicle, Francine never noticed the intense vibrations running throughout the bridge.

She did hear the awful wrenching sound.

"What was that?" she wondered aloud.

The Cordoba gave a massive bounce and flipped forward, its back end somersaulting up and over. It vanished.

Francine's mouth fell open. She slammed the brakes full-force. The car squealed to a halt at the edge of an open gap in the middle of the bridge.

She froze there, her hands clenched to the wheel. All of the traffic in front of her had disappeared.

Below, vehicles and chunks of asphalt rained into the river.

A sudden crunching force slammed into Francine's back bumper. Before it registered that another vehicle had struck her from behind, the blue Porsche sailed forward. Francine clung to the wheel and screamed.

The car spun through open air. Francine saw the dark sky spinning through the driver's side window, and then the even darker stretch of river rushing toward her below. She screamed until the Porsche hit the river and her world exploded into liquid and destruction. Another vehicle, the one that struck her from behind, came hurtling down on top of her.

IV

In the vacant Sharpe house, dishes rattled. Glasses shook in their cabinets. From one open cabinet, glasses fell and shattered against the kitchen countertop.

A small crack, previously undetected, began to spread. With a faint crackling sound and a puff of plaster dust, it opened from one tiny corner to spread halfway across the white wall of the kitchen.

A ceiling fan loosed from its anchoring and fell, the cord jerking taut. Within another moment, the fixture crashed to the floor. Its large bulb exploded in a scattering of glass.

In the study where Damon Sharpe had spent months poring over his work, papers fluttered from the desk into the floor. A book fell from a bookshelf before the shelves' bottom support succumbed and books cascaded down into a pile.

In the living room, another narrow crack snaked across the ceiling. The ceiling creaked, its cracks spreading, until it came apart.

Several cardboard boxes from the attic crashed down into the living room floor. The boxes split apart and photographs poured across the carpet.

V

One minute, Jake Grant drove over the River Bridge. The next, water submerged everything and his car became a water-filled steel prison.

He sucked in his next breath almost without thinking. The heavy dose of oxygen sustained him as he instinctively fought his way out. He pushed and kicked against the force that threatened to pull him down with the vehicle.

The river. He was in the river.

THE MOURNER'S CRADLE

A brief memory resurfaced in Jake's anxious mind, a story he once heard about the river's strange undercurrent which had claimed a few errant swimmers' lives in the past. Was it this pulling him down toward a watery death?

He fought to swim upward. The sun's light lent his only assurance of the river's surface. He swam with vigorous defiance for the light, getting closer and pushing harder until finally his head emerged from the water.

He gasped for oxygen. A clamor from somewhere behind frightened him, igniting reserves he hardly realized he had until now. Jake threw himself into immediate action, swimming for the river bank where numerous figures had gathered, some in uniforms.

When he neared the bank, the rescue personnel rushed to pull him out. They helped him to his feet, supported him when he almost fell, and eased him down. He sat on the ground, looked to the river, and watched the final vehicle sink beneath the water.

He struggled to fathom the occurrence. He remembered driving along the bridge before the world had vanished around him. He recalled the water and the harsh fight to escape, but that wasn't all. He couldn't look away from the surface of the water.

"What is it?" one of his rescuers, a bald firefighter with the stubble of a brown beard, asked.

Unable to find his voice, Jake's hands shook as he pointed toward the river. Deep below the surface, buried under mounds of wrecked automotive steel, his girlfriend of seven months floated in the watery tomb of his upside-down crushed sedan.

VI

A coffee cup rattled over the edge of the counter and dropped to the floor. It smashed into scattering ceramic pieces.

Detective C. J. Corbin looked up, startled. He stood from his rolling chair and found a towel. He threw the brown towel over the mess of coffee and ceramic and mopped it up with the sole of his boot.

In the middle of this task, his phone rang. He answered it. "This is Corbin," he spoke into the receiver.

"We need you up on the River Bridge, now." The chief's gruff urgency left no room for debate.

For the sake of preparation, Corbin had to ask, "What's the issue?"

"We've had a serious incident," the chief said. "The bridge gave out. We need every able body to get up there now. I'm counting on you."

The chief hung up. Corbin grabbed his jacket and hurried out the door.

When he arrived from downtown, traffic lights were backed up along both halves of the bridge. Blue lights and uniforms covered each side with the efforts to usher everyone from the bridge to safety.

Corbin couldn't get in with his vehicle, so he took to the River Bridge on foot as many others had. He hardly noticed the vibrations beneath his feet. Although these vibrations desisted, the panic among everyone fleeing the River Bridge hadn't subsided a bit.

"Corbin!" the chief shouted. Corbin ran over.

"I've got some of the others closing off the bridge," the chief said, casting quick eyes around. "I don't want anyone else going up there. They're saying this was an earthquake."

"An earthquake?" Corbin echoed, but the chief had already moved on to address the rest of the officers arriving on the scene.

Corbin ran for the bridge. Along the way, he heard the blaring of more sirens from police vehicles, ambulances, and fire trucks some distance behind.

VII

Mike Williams, wearing his usual blue button-up shirt and name tag, leaned against the front counter of the King's Motel. As the motel's manager for the past year or so, he worked the front desk often. No one else showed up for work two-thirds of the time.

When he felt the vibrations in the wooden front counter, he didn't react or even care until he saw multiple customers standing out in the motel's parking lot. A grudging interest prompted him to step outside.

He withdrew a cheap lighter, lit a cigarette, and smoked while listening to the other people babble on.

An earthquake? Here in St. Charles? That was something different. He wasn't sure whether he believed it yet.

A red Ferrari whipped into the parking lot. The vehicle braked when someone ran past the front end of the car. It resumed moving, more slowly this time, closing several more feet before stopping. The driver's side door flew open. A woman in a red dress, her hair wavy and brown, stepped out. She ran around the car.

"Anne, where are you?" she called. No one paid any attention to her.

She saw Mike leaning against the wall near the lobby door and came over. "Excuse me," she said. "Do you work here?"

"I'm on break," Mike said. "And in case you haven't noticed, things are kind of weird right now. Come back later."

"I'm looking for someone," the woman said. "Her name is Anne Sharpe. Is she staying here?"

"How would I know?" Mike slipped the cigarette back into his mouth.

"Because you work here. Look, she might be in trouble. She called me earlier—"

Mike extinguished his cigarette on the outer wall of the hotel and went back inside. The woman followed him in.

"I'm not leaving until you tell me something," she insisted.

"Fine," Mike said. "What's her name?"

The woman crossed her arms. "Anne Sharpe," she said.

Mike moved around the front counter, found a brown book, and consulted its pages. "Room 26," he said.

The woman walked out of the lobby. *About damned time,* Mike thought.

VIII

Once out of the motel's lobby, Tabby Reinhart hurried to Room 26. The door stood ajar. She looked inside.

"Anne!" she called. She pushed inside, switched on

THE MOURNER'S CRADLE

the light, and saw no one in the room. She moved to the bathroom door, but paused outside to knock.

"Hello? Anne? Are you in there?"

No response.

Tabby opened the door, glanced in and around the tiny bathroom to no avail, and headed back out to the parking lot. There she spoke up, drawing the attention of a few in the parking lot despite their chattering.

"Does anyone here know Anne Sharpe?"

People stared at her, blank-faced.

Tabby launched into a physical description. A heavyset, gray-haired man approached, holding up his hand.

"Ma'am? I think I remember seeing her. She stumbled off like she might have been drunk. She left already."

"Which way?" Tabby asked.

The man pointed down the street. "Thank you," Tabby said. She hopped back into her Ferrari, backed up, and left the parking lot.

She waited for an opening before reemerging onto the street. As she drove along, the radio pummeled her with news of the quake.

The River Bridge had come down. People were dying.

Tabby scanned the roadside for some sign of Anne. A figure ran across the street in front of her. She slammed her brakes, swerving left. Another vehicle, a van, lurched out from the left side. Tabby jerked the wheel back to the right. The Ferrari's front bumper struck the van and Tabby hit the windshield face-first.

She gasped, her heart thumping, blood running down her face. She slid down the steering wheel and collapsed into the seat. She grasped for the door's handle. It seemed to take minutes to find it.

"What's wrong with you, lady?" the van's driver bellowed. The pudgy man saw Tabby's face, and his narrow, furious eyes widened with surprise.

Her nose broken and her face covered with blood, she stumbled away from the vehicle and collapsed in the street amid a fanfare of shouts and car horns.

IX

In the King's Motel, Mike opened the door behind the lobby's counter. Inside the storage room, brown cardboard boxes of toilet paper, paper towels, cleaning agents, and other miscellaneous supplies flanked each side of the door. A working color television rested on another couple of boxes against the far wall. Mike walked over to switch it on. The news blared.

He closed the door and leaned against the cardboard boxes to watch the report. A sizable cockroach skittered past his feet. He flinched and stomped twice, but missed it. Before he could try again, it fled between the stacks of boxes.

Damn, that was a huge cockroach, he thought. *Oh, well.*

Mike went back to watching television. The front desk could probably do without him for a while.

The television showed multiple red-and-blue flashing lights near the downtown end of the River Bridge. Multiple police were on the premises, more than Mike had ever seen together at once. A reporter held a microphone and spoke into the camera.

"What we are witnessing," she said, "is an

earthquake of a magnitude St. Charles has never experienced. Authorities have determined that the River Bridge has sustained severe structural damage, and some vehicles have actually fallen into the river. Some are questioning the soundness of the bridge's structure prior to this disaster. There have been numerous casualties but the injury and death toll is still unknown. We have had reports from other areas of St. Charles, but so far, most of the damage has affected the bridge and the downtown area . . . "

MINUTE OF TRUTH

I

THE GROUND STEADIED across St. Charles. Mike Williams still sat in the storage room behind the front counter of the King's Motel, watching continued coverage of the earthquake's effects.

"Authorities have reported that the River Bridge has been closed due to the earthquake's destruction," the reporter said. "All around St. Charles, especially downtown, we continue to receive reports of damages. While many people around the city are working to pick up the pieces, a few have questioned the possibility of an aftershock. We'll have more on this later. We will also be on the scene with officers at the River Bridge for a full report on the additional difficulties this catastrophe could mean for the residents of St. Charles in the days and months ahead. Please stay tuned to this channel for further updates as they develop."

Around the River Bridge, blue lights whirled. Police guarded the River Bridge and turned away traffic as it arrived. Below, on both sides of the river, more officers worked to haul bodies from the water. Residents of nearby areas stood watching and talked among themselves.

The house of Damon and Anne Sharpe stood silent and fractured. Remnants of plaster dust and particles of dust and insulation from the attic settled across the carpet, furniture, and photographs from the broken boxes.

Beyond the black iron gates of Marion Cemetery, Anne slept on her husband's unmarked grave, her breathing faint. Through her darkened mind flashed the sight of her eyes in the mirror.

What should have remained buried in that distant pit of the mountain, she had found. She harbored it within and it was the deepest source of her suffering.

An object fell from her blouse. Her sleep dissolved, and she saw the open switchblade that had fallen.

She reached for it. Swallowing, she closed her eyes again, confronted the beast within, and exerted her will into the blade.

||

Across the barren mindscape of her dreamless sleep, Anne registered some indistinct nuance of the whispering in the cemetery. She heard soft footsteps, quiet like the gentlest wind across dead leaves.

The old gravedigger, Dominguez, approached. Behind him, the shadows stood still.

"Is it the endless sleep?" Dominguez mused. "She is covered in blood. What happened to her?"

The shadows remained silent as they often had, offering no answers, but still they followed Dominguez, observing and absorbing his words. Dominguez raised a hand to rub his coarse jaw.

"I am no stranger to death," he spoke in his

whisper, "but we have never seen the violence of murder here, have we? No, this is no murder. This is something else."

His old eyes finally saw the red blade in her loose fingers. "She has been cutting herself," he realized aloud.

He studied her breathing. However faint, her chest still moved. She still lived.

Accustomed to airing his thoughts in the presence of his shadows, Dominguez parted his dry, leathery lips to speak again, but stanched his words when Anne's eyes blinked open.

III

She thought she could see faces through her fog. She thought she could hear a voice whispering, and she saw the ruby ring.

"Help me," Anne said. She could no longer hold her eyes open.

"Please," she whispered once more, as no one had answered her. "There is something inside me."

Dominguez came closer.

"Please," she whispered again. Dominguez grasped the affliction within her voice, puzzled.

Something inside her? Indeed. He thought of the treasures that must still pulse with some life inside her, even if death hovered near.

His years as a medical professional were decades behind him. Of those months spent associating with a certain merchant of the black market organ trade and the subsequent loss of his status as a medical professional, Dominguez had spoken to no one save that man and the shadows that now accompanied him.

Still, his old curiosity remained. He could not deny it. The anatomy and workings of the human body had always fascinated him.

Dominguez came to her. His fingers stopped short of her blood-soaked blouse. The gash ran deep through her abdomen.

He looked into the opening she had forced, upward and to the side, with cold red metal. From this close, he could see it within her, the black, white, and yellow taint of an ages-dormant malignancy in the flesh.

He reached in. Blood welled. When he drew it out and saw it in full, he recoiled. He fell back, his heart pumping hard at the sight of the thing in his hands. Never in his ninety-nine years on earth had Dominguez ever witnessed such a sight.

He tried to stand again and found he could not. His breaths came short.

One of the shadows came down beside him, looking to assist. The other, one with the disguise of a painted face, gripped her shoulder.

"Look," red lips whispered from the white-painted face. "Look at it."

The shadows stared at it, motionless, until Dominguez held the thing up and delivered it into their arms.

"I need a moment," Dominguez faltered. "Just a moment."

He stood and ambled with slow steps to accompany them toward the gates.

Anne's eyes opened a fraction to witness their departure. Old Dominguez and the shadows fled toward the gates.

Anne drew on a faint memory of the old tales of Marion Cemetery. Yes, she knew of those faded stories of the shadows as Damon had known of them, but she had never seen the cemetery shadows for herself until this night.

Now the shadows carried that horrible thing away, she saw, and she hoped they would carry it far and bury it so deep no one would ever find it again.

She felt no malice, no more fury—only a sense of absence. She closed her eyes to the world. She faded and settled into the silence of eternity.

Dominguez fell against the cemetery's iron gate. His heartbeat became erratic, worse. His chest tightened.

"Leave me," he whispered to the shadows at last. "My days are done."

The shadows hurried from the cemetery. Dominguez made slow steps to Cemetery Road, found one of its trees, and slumped against it. He put his hands to his chest. In time, he crumpled.

Leaving Cemetery Road, the shadows merged into the darkness of the downtown city streets.

In their arms, a nameless spawn of sorrows stared from yellow, dead slits of eyes. For the days and months to come, it would serve to remind the shadows that, on this strange night of '79, they were close to something great until death itself intervened to push them away.

With the dead thing in their arms between them, they fled the city streets for a place darker yet, where they belonged, where it belonged, and they were gone.

TRAGEDY

I

AT THE FRONT desk of the King's Motel, Mike Williams read a newspaper, absorbing further second-hand details of the quake's impact along with all of the latest sports updates. The maid came in to work as usual but shrank away from cleaning one of the rooms. The guest there had screamed at her like a lunatic, she claimed.

Annoyed, Mike dropped the newspaper and stood up. Since the maid couldn't be bothered to do her job today, it fell on his shoulders.

He snatched the maid's cart from her and wheeled it to the room. The door stood slightly open, he noticed. He knocked. No one answered.

"Anybody in there?" he called. He allowed five seconds for a response before he pushed the red door wide open and walked in.

The room was vacant. The comforter lay halfway off the bed. The sheets were wrinkled.

The clock radio on the bedside nightstand blared the news. He almost switched it off, but decided not to bother. At least it gave him something to listen to while he took his time with a task he didn't feel like doing.

He noticed the worn green pack on the floor beside the bed. He peeked inside and saw papers bunched within. Most of it was trash, he guessed. He threw the supply pack onto the cart. He would toss it in the lost-and-found box. If no one showed up to claim it soon, it would go into the trash dumpster.

He pulled the comforter from the bed and peeled the sheets off. He shoved the wadded sheets into a bag. He stopped for a brief bathroom break and washed his hands before coming back to wrap up the cleaning.

The radio kept playing in the background. Instead of music or some disc jockey's inane banter as might be the case any other day, there continued more reports of the previous day's tragedy.

Mike briefly wondered about the room's occupant. He couldn't remember her name, though he had looked at her information before, he was sure, because he remembered that annoying woman coming in to demand it.

She hadn't checked out or renewed her stay. She had left her things here, but they appeared to be worthless.

With a glance back at the dusty olive-green pack, the motel's manager mumbled, "Well, whatever."

He continued to clean and tidy up the room. The radio's reports drifted in and out.

"It's a terrible tragedy that has hit St. Charles within the past day—"

"More bodies were recovered—"

"Police are still searching for survivors—"

Mike switched off the radio, loaded the cart, and rolled it away. He saw the maid cleaning another room and stopped to lean in.

In the middle of changing the pillowcases, the maid glanced up when Mike's head popped around the corner.

"Room 26 is empty," he threw curtly at her. He left the cart by the open doorway and returned to the front desk. He tapped his fingers on the desk for another minute before deciding he needed a cigarette.

Later in the day, he heard a brief mention of Anne Sharpe's death on the news. They found her next to the grave of her own husband, the late researcher Damon Sharpe. A few in St. Charles remembered Mr. Sharpe, but not many knew his wife.

Another unidentified body was discovered somewhere on the side of the road outside the cemetery, beneath one of the elm trees.

Few other details were released. A police investigation had launched, but given the crisis of the earthquake, the efforts of an investigation would likely be scant.

Anne was buried in Marion Cemetery next to her husband. Both graves were unmarked.

Mike didn't remember her name, and didn't make the connection. People came and went in his line of work. He seldom remembered any of them.

"It was a tragedy," some might have said before moving onto another topic.

Mike Williams wouldn't have agreed. The quake was a tragedy. Numerous lives were lost. Families would grieve. Homes would have to be rebuilt. The River Bridge had come down.

A single death such as Anne Sharpe's was just another Tuesday.

II

Tabby rested in her home. A large white bandage covered her nose, a gift from the hospital after her accident. The television rambled on, but it was noise to her.

Most of her friends stayed with their families during this time. Anne hadn't had a family, except for Damon, Tabby knew. Tabby had only her father who lived several hundred miles away and her sister in California whom she never saw and seldom spoke to.

She wondered if they had heard the news of the quake. The phone hadn't rang.

Tabby received the news of Anne's death from among the rest of the news reports, most focusing on the disaster. She wasn't sure how she felt about that. If she thought about it much longer, she feared she might understand all too well how she felt about it.

She opened her prescription bottle, popped a pain pill, and washed it down with a sip of warm mint tea from a petite ceramic cup, once one of a set until the others fell and broke into white pieces across her kitchen counter.

Tabby slumped into the cushions of her white sofa. Her eyes fell on the television. News of the quake kept repeating itself until she had to get up and change the channel.

What a nightmare, she thought, dropping back onto the sofa. *But that's life,* as her father would say.

III

A few things changed after the quake, most noticeably in the heart of the city's downtown portion—the King's Motel, Summerset Park, the clustered bars, nightclubs, and ramshackle shops packed into Candle Square, and even Marion Cemetery. The whispers had ceased, and it had become a quiet place.

That bleak day of the Quake of '79 was the day everything changed, some would reflect in the years to come. It was the day St. Charles lost its innocence.

Business picked up at the King's Motel and many of the city's other hotels and motels. Those who had lost homes to the quake needed places to sleep. Some found assistance, but not all, and with this, lodging cashed in on a natural catastrophe.

There was an alley behind the King's Motel. Mike Williams did his best to keep it clean, but wanderers regularly littered and pissed in it. There had been a rash of vandals lately, evidenced by the recent spurts of graffiti. He didn't see anyone there on the evening he heaved the unclaimed green supply pack into the trash dumpster.

Dusk drew near. It was as good of a time as any for a cigarette, Mike thought, and lit up another one.

ABOUT THE AUTHOR

Tommy B. Smith is a writer of dark fiction and the author of *Poisonous,* as well as the short story collection *Pieces of Chaos,* and of course, *The Mourner's Cradle.* His work has appeared in numerous publications over the years to include *Every Day Fiction, Night to Dawn,* and the anthology *Tales from The Lake Vol. 3.* His presence currently infests Fort Smith, Arkansas, where he resides with his wife and cats.

More information can be found on his website at http://www.tommybsmith.com.

THE END?

Not quite . . .

Dive into more Tales from the Darkest Depths:

Novels:
House of Sighs (with sequel novella) by Aaron Dries
Beyond Night by Eric S. Brown and Steven L. Shrewsbury
The Third Twin: A Dark Psychological Thriller by Darren Speegle
Aletheia: A Supernatural Thriller by J.S. Breukelaar
Beatrice Beecham's Cryptic Crypt: A Supernatural Adventure/Mystery Novel by Dave Jeffery
Where the Dead Go to Die by Mark Allan Gunnells and Aaron Dries
Sarah Killian: Serial Killer (For Hire!) by Mark Sheldon
The Final Cut by Jasper Bark
Blackwater Val by William Gorman
Pretty Little Dead Girls: A Novel of Murder and Whimsy by Mercedes M. Yardley
Nameless: The Darkness Comes by Mercedes M. Yardley

Novellas:
A Season in Hell by Kenneth W. Cain
Quiet Places: A Novella of Cosmic Folk Horror by Jasper Bark

The Final Reconciliation by Todd Keisling
Run to Ground by Jasper Bark
Devourer of Souls by Kevin Lucia
Apocalyptic Montessa and Nuclear Lulu: A Tale of Atomic Love by Mercedes M. Yardley
Wind Chill by Patrick Rutigliano
Little Dead Red by Mercedes M. Yardley
Sleeper(s) by Paul Kane
Stuck On You by Jasper Bark

Anthologies:
Welcome to The Show, edited by Doug Murano
Lost Highways: Dark Fictions From the Road, edited by D. Alexander Ward
C.H.U.D. Lives! – A Tribute Anthology
Tales from The Lake Vol.4: The Horror Anthology, edited by Ben Eads
Behold! Oddities, Curiosities and Undefinable Wonders, edited by Doug Murano
Twice Upon an Apocalypse: Lovecraftian Fairy Tales, edited by Rachel Kenley and Scott T. Goudsward
Tales from The Lake Vol.3, edited by Monique Snyman
Gutted: Beautiful Horror Stories, edited by Doug Murano and D. Alexander Ward
Tales from The Lake Vol.2, edited by Joe Mynhardt, Emma Audsley, and RJ Cavender
Children of the Grave
The Outsiders
Tales from The Lake Vol.1, edited by Joe Mynhardt
Fear the Reaper, edited by Joe Mynhardt
For the Night is Dark, edited by Ross Warren

Short story collections:
Frozen Shadows and Other Chilling Stories by Gene O'Neill
Varying Distances by Darren Speegle
The Ghost Club: Newly Found Tales of Victorian Terror by William Meikle
Ugly Little Things: Collected Horrors by Todd Keisling
Whispered Echoes by Paul F. Olson
Embers: A Collection of Dark Fiction by Kenneth W. Cain
Visions of the Mutant Rain Forest, by Bruce Boston and Robert Frazier
Tribulations by Richard Thomas
Eidolon Avenue: The First Feast by Jonathan Winn
Flowers in a Dumpster by Mark Allan Gunnells
The Dark at the End of the Tunnel by Taylor Grant
Through a Mirror, Darkly by Kevin Lucia
Things Slip Through by Kevin Lucia
Where You Live by Gary McMahon
Tricks, Mischief and Mayhem by Daniel I. Russell
Samurai and Other Stories by William Meikle
Stuck On You and Other Prime Cuts by Jasper Bark

Poetry collections:
WAR by Alessandro Manzetti and Marge Simon
Brief Encounters with My Third Eye by Bruce Boston
No Mercy: Dark Poems by Alessandro Manzetti
Eden Underground: Poetry of Darkness by Alessandro Manzetti

If you've ever thought of becoming an author, we'd also like to recommend these non-fiction titles:

Where Nightmares Come From: The Art of Storytelling in the Horror Genre, edited by Joe Mynhardt and Eugene Johnson
Horror 101: The Way Forward, edited by Joe Mynhardt and Emma Audsley
Horror 201: The Silver Scream Vol.1 and *Vol.2*, edited by Joe Mynhardt and Emma Audsley
Modern Mythmakers: 35 interviews with Horror and Science Fiction Writers and Filmmakers by Michael McCarty
Writers On Writing: An Author's Guide Volumes 1,2,3, and 4, edited by Joe Mynhardt. Now also available in a Kindle and paperback omnibus.

Or check out other Crystal Lake Publishing books for more Tales from the Darkest Depths. Or follow us on Patreon for behind the scenes access.

Hi, readers. It makes our day to know you reached the end of our book. Thank you so much. This is why we do what we do every single day.

Whether you found the book good or great, we'd love to hear what you thought. Please take a moment to leave a review on Amazon, Goodreads, or anywhere else readers visit. Reviews go a long way to helping a book sell, and will help us to continue publishing quality books. You can also share a photo of yourself holding this book with the hashtag #IGotMyCLPBook!

Thank you again for taking the time to journey with Crystal Lake Publishing.

We are also on . . .

Website:
www.crystallakepub.com

Be sure to sign up for our newsletter and receive two free eBooks: http://eepurl.com/xfuKP

Books:
http://www.crystallakepub.com/book-table/

Twitter:
https://twitter.com/crystallakepub

Facebook:
https://www.facebook.com/Crystallakepublishing/
https://www.facebook.com/Talesfromthelake/
https://www.facebook.com/WritersOnWritingSeries/

Pinterest:
https://za.pinterest.com/crystallakepub/

Instagram:
https://www.instagram.com/crystal_lake_publishing/

Patreon:
https://www.patreon.com/CLP

YouTube:
https://www.youtube.com/c/CrystalLakePublishing

We'd love to hear from you.

Or check out other Crystal Lake Publishing books for your Dark Fiction, Horror, Suspense, and Thriller needs.

With unmatched success since 2012, Crystal Lake Publishing has quickly become one of the world's leading indie publishers of Mystery, Thriller, and Suspense books with a Dark Fiction edge.

Crystal Lake Publishing puts integrity, honor and respect at the forefront of our operations.

We strive for each book and outreach program that's launched to not only entertain and touch or comment on issues that affect our readers, but also to strengthen and support the Dark Fiction field and its authors.

Not only do we publish authors who are legends in the field and as hardworking as us, but we look for men and women who care about their readers and fellow human beings. We only publish the very best Dark Fiction, and look forward to launching many new careers.

We strive to know each and every one of our readers, while building personal relationships with our authors, reviewers, bloggers, pod-casters, bookstores and libraries.

Crystal Lake Publishing is and will always be a beacon of what passion and dedication, combined with overwhelming teamwork and respect, can accomplish: Unique fiction you can't find anywhere else.

We do not just publish books, we present you worlds within your world, doors within your mind, from talented authors who sacrifice so much for a moment of your time.

This is what we believe in. What we stand for. This will be our legacy.

Welcome to Crystal Lake Publishing—Tales from the Darkest Depths

CPSIA information can be obtained
at www.ICGtesting.com
Printed in the USA
FSHW02n1804191018
52976FS